Since her parents became grey nomads, Queenie Hart was just about alone in the world. Her strange obsession with all things Scottish in the weeks before Halloween was ruining her life. While in the grip of the Caledonian Curse, she insulted people and spent money she couldn't afford on bagpipe serenades. She turned down a date with her perfect man, angered her employers, and pushed her landlady into giving her notice. She, and her little baking business *Queen of Tarts*, would soon be homeless.

Queenie's luck changed when her dad's odd cousin found her a rent-free home for three months. The Belfry was a converted church, and Queenie was soon embroiled with the attractive but married landlord, and a man she knew as the Fixer. The Fixer helped her whenever she needed . . . but Halloween was coming, Caledonia was calling, and it was so the wrong time be starting on a new romance.

Queen of Tarts 1

ISBN: 978-1-4874-3450-2
Cover art by Martine Jardin

Published by eXtasy Books Inc

Look for us online at:
www.eXtasybooks.com

Queen of Tarts 1
A Fairy in the Bed

By

Lark Westerly

Dedication

In loving memory of my grandmother, who made tarts and loved all things Scottish.

Author's Note:

The *Fairy in the Bed* series features a sprawling cast of characters who wander in and out of one another's stories.

Queenie Hart is a new character, but you might recognise some of the supporting players from other books in the series.

Queen of Tarts takes place in 2020 and 2021, but for the purposes of this story, the Covid 19 epidemic never happened. After all, it's not *quite* our world.

For more about the series, visit Lark's website at https://larksinger.weebly.com

Chapter One: Fairings

Jacaranda Fairling, October 25th, 2021

Jacaranda Fairling was seldom surprised by what her clients wanted. Indeed, in her twenty-five years of trading in Lady Lane she thought she'd heard it all, from the awkward teenager who needed a green dress, *now,* for a social *tonight,* to a bride who wanted rainbows and a place to store her dog for half an hour.

Come to think of it, those had been the same person, a decade or so apart.

Then there'd been the woman who'd fancied a vintage party dress so she wouldn't look like a mother-of-the-bride, even though she was . . .

Jacaranda liked to think she was a good judge of what would suit a walk-in, but there was something *off* about this one.

"You're not twins, are you?" she asked abruptly.

The would-be customer looked confused.

Jacaranda answered herself. "No, of course you're not."

"Only child," the client said in a soft, low voice, speaking precisely as if auditioning for a part.

"What do you think, Lu?" Jacaranda glanced at her partner, Lucida, who was fey as well as fay. Lucida, as usual, looked to be away with the fairies, but her soft startled doe's eyes glanced sideways in a smile, and she gave a tiny nod. She approved of the idea, or possibly of the customer. It was difficult to be sure, with Lu.

Oh, why not?

Jacaranda faced her puzzling client. "I expect we could manage that. It would make a change from all the Wicked Wiles costumes I've been asked to make this month. There's only so much one can do with black cloaks and tall hats, but I suppose it's the obvious costume for *Wicked Wiles*-themed Halloween parties."

"Tarts and hearts aren't wicked," Lucida said, directly to the stranger.

"Och, I know that, but you see—it's advertising," the client explained. She was a tall, full-figured young woman with a mass of wavy strawberry-blonde hair. Her Scottish accent came and went, so she sounded like a bad actor.

That's what it is. She's acting some of the time. But which voice is real, and which is the act?

Jacaranda said, "I'll see you on Friday afternoon, then."

"That's cutting it a wee bit fine."

"It's the best I can do, Ms Hart. Until then I'll be elbow-deep in black crepe. Of course, you could always pop around to *Thrifty Buys*."

"*Lawks!*" The client looked horrified. "I wouldnae be seen deid in junk from there."

Deid . . . What was this? Robbie Burns Night?

Jacaranda raised her eyebrows. "I know a woman who got a fairy doll there for her Christmas tree a few years back. She paid a fiver for it."

"And it fell apart? Burst into flames? Said something verra inappropriate to a gueist?"

Lucida laughed suddenly, then clapped her hands over her mouth. Her eyes, usually mournful and uncertain, danced with merriment.

Jacaranda cleared her throat. "There were no guests involved, but I believe it—he—*did* say something inappropriate to Frances. But Frances has still got it. Him."

"*Him?*"

"Fairies can be *hims*. And this one was."

It was decidedly a *him*, with every *him* attribute a betrayed and angry girl could want. That was if what Jacaranda had heard was true, and she had no reason to believe it wasn't.

"Obviously, fairies can be laddies," the client said. She added, thoughtfully, having wrestled her accent into submission, "Speaking of *hims* . . . do you think this costume might—um—please a laddie? To keep the lang-leggedy beasties at bay on Halloween night?"

"You can bank on it." The words were out of Jacaranda's mouth before she could hold them back.

The customer looked pleased. "Namaste." She put her palms together and bent her head for a moment.

Then she went out under the tinkle of shop bells.

Jacaranda said, under her breath, "Though whether *one* laddie is enough for you is another matter . . ."

Why did I say that? Is it the feeling that she ought to be twins?

"Namaste?" Lucida asked.

"It means the same as *greet you*, more or less, only you can use it for goodbyes as well as hellos," Jacaranda said. She frowned. "But you're right. It doesn't compute. Doesn't go with all that Scotchness. Scotsness. Scottishness?"

Lucida lifted a hand and used her forefinger to make a small circle in the air near her temple. In anyone else, Jacaranda would have considered this a vulgar and rude gesture, but Lucida Castleby was never vulgar or rude. She never raised her voice, and she was never unkind, despite all the unkindness that had once been done to her.

Jacaranda looked at her business partner with affection. There was no use asking Lu what she meant by that odd gesture. She seldom replied to a direct question.

"Maybe we'll find out what it's all about one day," she said.

Or maybe not.

"Lu," she said abruptly, "how would you feel about

driving up the coast to a Halloween Ball? Would Lindon care to come?"

Lucida tilted her head, as if listening to something far away. "I do love music. Maybe Lindon would like to dance."

Jacaranda thought Lindon Castleby would like anything to please his Lucida. She had never seen a husband more in love with his wife.

"Ash and Jessie should come, too," Lucida said, nodding.

Jacaranda saw she'd need to consider costumes for a party of six.

Chapter Two: The Caledonian Curse

Queenie Hart, October 31st, 2021. Halloween

Queenie Hart hitched herself into her Halloween costume, one boob at a time, and glanced down at her impressive cleavage.

She assessed her reflection in the tall looking glass, her gaze shifting from her Victorian button boots up her long legs to the top of her puffed up hair.

"No' a tartan in sight. Ye'll do, lassie," she remarked.

She caught herself up and grimaced. That dastardly dialect always sneaked up on her at this time of the year. From November to September, she kept it at bay with no more than a tiny mental filter. The tartan tammy and the skirl of bagpipes, the waft of heather and the sudden desire for sporrans and laddies in kilts and a birch besom—she was familiar with them all—but it was a problem only in October. No one had been able to explain it fully to her, although she had a better understanding now than she'd had a year ago. Most people thought she was putting it on or doing it to annoy. It had got her two recommendations for therapy and one failed aptitude test and had probably cost her at least two jobs. Her only two semi-serious boyfriends had given up on her. She had tried self-managed aversion therapy with a rubber band, meditation, hibernation, and pretending it didn't exist. Hibernation was the only treatment that sort of worked, but that wasn't always practical.

She called it *the Caledonian Curse.*

Last year, the Curse had almost got her into serious trouble. This year it had pushed away someone whose good opinion she valued. Now, she was hoping her desperate measures might save her bacon. Or did she mean her scotch broth?

Faint heart never won fair laddie . . .

Though, to be sure, the laddie was hers for the asking. It was the other one, the one whose face was a mystery to her, that might cause her some problems.

She touched the extravagantly lovely thistle pendant that dangled *just so* from its red gold chain.

Should I hae accepted this? Och, but how could I hae disappointed him, again?

This was going to be tricky, she knew, and she had just this one Halloween night to pull it off.

Chapter Three: Living Statue

Queenie Hart. October 30th, 2020.

A year and a day before hitching her boobs into her Halloween costume, Queenie was holed up in her unit in Mother Goose Lane writing a post for her baking blog, *Queen of Tarts.*

Mother Goose Lane sounded an intriguing address, but the unit was far from the nursery rhyme cottage its name implied. It was one of four identical buildings. The landlady, Angel Petty, lived in one of them, one was rented to a FIFO worker, and the third was inhabited by a woman who knitted and made pizza. That was about all Queenie knew about her. She had never responded to any of Queenie's tentative overtures.

Possibly that had to do with the bagpipe serenade Queenie had accidentally arranged for herself the first Halloween of her tenure in Mother Goose Lane.

Bagpipes aside, it was a quiet place to live.

Halloween loomed again. Her latest boyfriend had drifted off some weeks ago, so Queenie was distracting herself with thoughts of food and revenue. It was four weeks since she'd been able to take a shift at any of the part time jobs she had. The annoyance her employers displayed when she refused October shifts was nothing to the way they'd react if she showed up and abused a customer in a flood of incomprehensible Gaelic or, worse, a cod Scotch broth of invective.

It was bad enough dealing with the landlady, the sleekit auld besom.

Och! One of these days ye'll term her that to her heid.

Despite her precautions, she lost focus on her recipes and drifted off to the place she termed *Caledonia-on-my-mind.*

When she regained control of her brain, she was horrified to realise she was on the *Fly Me Now* website, in the act of purchasing a round trip ticket to Scotland. *Book Now!* shrieked the flashing advertisement.

Her finger hovered a breath away from the key that would finalise the purchase. She had only to hit that enticing *Book Now!* and she'd be pledging over twenty-two hundred dollars for a trip to a place she'd never been and where, so far as she knew, she had no ties—and that was before she figured in accommodation and other expenses.

The worst aspect was that she had the twenty-two hundred dollars in her rent fund, ready for automatic direct debit, so the payment would go through instantly . . .

Och noo ye dinnae.

She grabbed her right hand in her left and dragged it back, then hurriedly X-ed out of the site. "What the feck are ye *doing,* ye daft lassie?" she demanded of herself. Her voice was redolent of peat fires, tartan and stags-in-the-heather.

She closed the laptop with a snap and scooted away from the desk. She shot out into the fresh air in case she was tempted again. On the way through the minute kitchen, she knocked over a sifter of flour and dropped her mobile on the kitchen draining board. Too bad if it skidded into the sink or choked on powdered wheat. She was out of here!

Queenie caught a train to Circular Quay and went for a walk, taking in the scents and sights and sounds of a Sydney spring morning. She was desperate to avoid sliding back into Scottishness and falling victim to the Caledonian Curse.

She drew in a big breath of relief as she watched gulls and heard the toot of a ferry.

A living statue bowed to her, extending his hat in slow motion. Instead of the usual formal or clownish attire affected by these performers, this one wore drawstring linen pants, a hip-length top laced at the neck, and soft shoes. His cap was empty, without even seed money, so she dug in her pocket and tossed him a scatter of coins, which was all she had with her.

She felt for anyone scraping by with part time work and ingenious enterprise. It was what she did herself.

"Good luck," she murmured.

That was what she intended, anyhow. Unfortunately, it came out as, "Lang may yer lum reek," in accents rich with rolling Rs.

The statue slowly withdrew his cap, peeped in and then, as slowly, extended it again.

"Hoots, mannie!" Queenie exclaimed. She closed her eyes and bit her lip.

Stop it with the Scottishness!

When she opened her eyes again, the coins were gone and there was a snip of tartan cloth in the hat.

Queenie stared at it.

The statue, whose face was painted an unlikely green, gave her a slow-motion nod and a smile.

"For your kindness, bonnie lassie," he whispered.

Queenie took the cloth and unfolded it to reveal the embroidered words, *One wish to make/ the road to take.*

She smiled. The statue was double-checking the *no begging* box. Her few coins were buying his performance and a physical item . . . to whit, a scrap of cloth.

The point was . . . how did one make a wish in this case? If she returned the cloth to him with the wish written on it, then she would not have the physical item . . .

Fash me! Sodding bylaws. Nyaff roasters.

That aside, what did she have to wish for?

To rid herself of the Caledonian Curse?

To make her landlady, Angel Petty, less . . . petty?

For a loving companion who would want her, Caledonia

Calling and all?

I could get a wee dog if that sleekit bitch hadnae forbid it.

All her wishes were either impossible or too close to her heart, so she dropped a curtsy in slow motion.

"That's gey guid o' ye, laddie, so I wish ye guid fortune and sweet dreams o' the nicht an' luck an' loe to attend ye for aye. Aye, and here's a wee bitty token to help ye on yer way."

She felt in her pocket for more coins, but she had none. Her fingers closed instead on one of her courtesy cards with her website address and she dropped it in his cap.

Ask for a free sample – queen of tarts.

He inched to examine the card and a thirty-second-long smile mesmerised her.

He blew her a slow-motion kiss and then returned to his statue self.

Queenie was heartened by the small interaction. It had reminded her that she wasn't the only one for whom life could be a struggle.

At least she had a place to live and a marketable skill, even though the two things seemed sometimes mutually exclusive.

Chapter Four: James Stuart

Queenie Hart. October 30th, 2020.

Queenie relaxed. She was a long way from the nearest website and nowhere near a physical travel agent. Her phone, her wallet, and her credit cards were back at the unit in Mother Goose Lane. Her three-six-five was on its lanyard around her neck, so her ride home was safe.

As she exhaled, she caught a young man staring at her chest. He had red-brown hair tied back in a tail, grey eyes the colour of a loch in winter, an argyle sweater in blue and grey, and pale clear skin that suggested he came from somewhere colder than Sydney.

He was exactly her type. Just the thing to warm her on those long October nights.

"Aye?" She felt breathless as her knees turned to jelly and her insides liquified.

He gestured towards her boobs.

Queenie snapped out of it.

He's going to grope me? In broad daylight? In public?

She gave him her most menacing glare as the Caledonian Curse flared to a fine blaze.

"Lay one finger on these titties, ye mingin' jimmy, and I'll have yer baws in a jar and your wee willie for me haggis . . ."

He flinched and withdrew his hand in a hurry. "I was just saying you've got flour on your—er—chest."

Lord, he had a Glaswegian accent.

Given there were about a hundred and twenty thousand

Scottish-born Australians in the country, the odds of meeting one at Circular Quay weren't all that low, but Queenie shied away, hot with embarrassment.

He smirked at her in confusion and held his hands up as if surrendering.

They gazed at one another for a few seconds and then he reached slowly into his pocket and withdrew a white handkerchief.

Who carries a handkerchief these days?

He waved it gently—a makeshift flag of truce.

She pulled her scattered wits together and she said, slowly, "I'm a pastrycook, laddie. Flour across the titties goes with the job."

His smirk deepened, and he offered the handkerchief. "Best brush it off, though. You'll upset the gluten-free brigade if you pollute their airspace. Unless that's potato flour or some other gluten-free option?"

"Noo, it's wheat."

"This is clean." He flapped the handkerchief again.

Queenie took it and brushed at herself, and a small cloud of flour sifted down.

"That's better," the man said, reclaiming the cloth square. His smirk changed to a genuine smile. "If you thought I was being a bit too personal there, I apologise. Obviously, you won't know my face. I'm James Stuart."

"The king or the actor?" she blurted.

He tucked the handkerchief in his pocket. "Neither. I get that reaction a lot. Would it help if I wore a man bun and grew a bushy beard? Not that that would be too easy for me."

"My name's Queenie," she said, holding out her hand.

He took it gently in his. "Queen of the May? Queen of my heart?"

"Queen of Tarts. That's my wee business, but my name really is Queenie. My parents were wishfu' to honour my four great-grannies, Victoria, Elizabeth, Mary and Adelaide. They couldnae agree on the order of the names, so they went with the compromise and honoured the lot in one go."

He laughed. "Now we're introduced, we could get a cold one or something. That's what Aussies drink, right? Though you're not an Aussie?"

Maybe he saw the withdrawal in her expression, for he released her hand. "The O-Quay Café does great coffee. Maybe tea. Bitter lemon. Chai. Celery juice from a Berry-Berry-Nice Juice Bar. You choose. I'll pay. Please say you'll come."

She held up her hand to stop him. "Thanks, laddie, but I'm awa'—" She broke off. *Awa' hame* would have sounded like an invitation. She'd love to take him home, but the Caledonian Curse would—well, she couldn't risk it. One disgraceful outburst was more than enough.

"Fine." He sounded disappointed. "Maybe our planets will align next time I'm here. Lovely to know you, Queenie. Remember me until we do meet again."

"Fare thee well, James Stuart."

She hurried off, shaken and disappointed.

I liked him. I might have really *liked him. Nice hands. Nice voice. Eccentric mindset.*

If it hadn't been so close to Halloween, if he hadn't been Scottish, if she hadn't almost bought an unintentional trip to Edinburgh, she would have said *yes* to that light-hearted invitation and hoped something might develop.

He was just what she'd have ordered . . . except maybe for the cords and argyle sweater.

A kilt would be just the ticket.

But she'd said *no*, and now she regretted it.

What harm could it do? I already skelped him with words and he didnae flee.

She turned quickly and scanned the locals and visitors walking on the waterfront, but James Stuart had disappeared. He might have hopped on a ferry or lost himself in the warren of narrow streets heading into The Rocks. Maybe he'd gone to the O-Quay Café.

Maybe he never existed.

But surely if I'd imagined him, I'd have gone the whole haggis and put him in that kilt.

She whimpered gently. Only a proper Scotsman could wear a kilt without looking like a poser. James Stuart would have been a natural.

Chapter Five: Need to Leave

Queenie Hart. October 31st, 2020 – August 2021

Halloween 2020 crept past in a blur of regrets and a lingering desire for thistles, castles, and a walk by the Clyde.

Queenie holed up in her postage-stamp kitchen, baking tarts for next week's market, with her laptop safely stored in the crawlspace in the ceiling. That wouldn't prevent her from retrieving it if she went into a Caledonian fugue, but with luck she'd come to her senses before a Curse-inspired impulse had her buy a case of fine scotch whiskey imported from Islay.

Once she woke safely into November, with eleven months before the Caledonian Curse overtook her again, she went back to Circular Quay. She didn't go so far as to dust herself with flour, but she wore the same outfit, and wandered about for an hour keeping an eye out for tied-back hair, loch-grey eyes, and lanky legs in or out of kilts.

She listened for the complex tones of a real Glaswegian accent.

James Stuart! I'm flour-free today, and the planets have aligned. I have a pocketful of courtesy cards for you to redeem, one tart at a time. Is that invitation for a cold one still on the table?

It was too much to hope she'd meet him again.

I should have given him *the courtesy card instead of wasting it on the statue. He might have turned up at my market stall for tarts.*

Maybe the living statue had another wish on offer? This time, she might use it selfishly.

But he wasn't there, either.

Over the next three months she spent quite a lot of time loitering at the quay. She'd go to the market, hitching a lift with her finger-puppet-making acquaintance, Lin, and, with her tarts all sold and her stock of cards depleted, she'd head to the quay for coffee.

The O-Quay café staff got to know her by name.

Your usual, Queenie?

Yes, thanks. A clear of the throat. *I was hoping to meet my friend here. James Stuart. Tall, hair tied back, grey eyes . . . argyle sweater? Well, maybe not the sweater. It's a bit hot for that.*

Sorry, haven't seen anyone like that today.

Have you seen him at all? I know he comes in here.

We're really not supposed –

God! They thought she was stalking him!

I understand. If he comes in, please remember me to him.

When the tourism season really kicked off, the O-Quay Café bulged with standing room only. Queenie, aware she probably *was* stalking the delectable Glaswegian, gave up.

What are you like? Hanging about looking for a man you encountered a grand total of once.

But that's the point. I need to know if he's the way I perceived him while I was under the Curse. He's probably quite ordinary without the Caledonian specs in place.

A quick search of social media and Link-Me turned up dozens of people named James Stuart . . . or it might have been Stewart. None of the James Stuarts or Stewarts on Link-Me was looking for *Queenie.*

He knew her first name, but why would he bother searching for a woman named Queenie who had chattered cod-Scotch at him and given him the brush-off after he tried to brush *her* off?

He wouldn't. All that *remember me* stuff was probably Caledonian-inspired imagination.

The O-Quay Café folk had probably warned him about her, anyway.

He might not live in Sydney. He could easily have been a visitor from another state or from overseas. That direct-from-Clydeside accent suggested he hadn't been long in Australia. He was probably back at home, doing whatever Glaswegians did in the northern winter, with some bonnie lassie who spoke properly twelve months of the year.

Queenie, uneasily aware that Obsession might well become her second middle name, decided to force the issue and remove herself from temptation.

No more Circular Quay.

No more O-Quay Café.

No more stalking the beautiful but possibly imaginary James Stuart.

That determination gave her the extra push she needed to get out of the unit with the inadequate kitchen and litigious landlady who was angry about ants and who accused her—quite rightly—of running a profitable enterprise from a residential building. She must get a place of her own.

She couldn't afford anything remotely big enough near the CBD. She probably couldn't afford anything in the city at all. She hadn't even found the Mother Goose Lane unit herself. She had fallen into it when a then-workmate needed someone to share the rent. Chey had left ages ago, and she should have left too.

She cruised websites, asked friends for leads, and answered advertisements for share-accommodation.

None of them fancied a roommate bent on baking dozens of tarts on Fridays.

She'd have to get right out of town.

Her finger-puppet acquaintance pointed out that a speciality tart business might not be the best fit for a rural location.

"At least you're close to the markets here."

"Yes, but my landlady has started inspecting me whenever she even imagines she smells baking. She just barges right in."

"You could have her for harassment."

"And she can have *me* for commercial enterprise."

"Well, get a full-time job and just bake for fun." Finger-Puppet Lin clearly had her own issues. Queenie realised she was stretching the lukewarm friendship as it was, relying on the other woman for transport to the market. She *did* chip in petrol money and give her tarts, but she supposed it must in inconvenient for Lin to leave home fifteen minutes earlier to make the detour to Mother Goose Lane.

"Never mind," she said wearily.

She resolved not to mention the thing again. If she found a place, she would let Lin know she no longer needed transport. They would both be relieved.

She went to information evenings that purported to teach her the secrets of getting into the property market.

She sought full-time positions that allowed her to work from home during October.

She emerged from this intensive activity convinced that what she wanted was all but impossible.

She had just one more string to her bow. She hadn't used it before, because it was the last straw, the final possibility, and because she knew it was probably hopeless.

She would pay a visit to her dad's Cousin Branok.

Chapter Six: Call on a Cousin

Queenie Hart. August 2021

No one would ever have taken Shane Hart and Branok St Ives for cousins. Shane was what Queenie's mum affectionately termed *blokey.* He was open and friendly, and he liked a good pub argument as much as the next man. He had strong opinions and he wore them, and his big heart, on his sleeve. He was four years older than Branok, but although they'd lived in the same general area until Queenie was nineteen, she had met the St Ives branch of the family only a handful of times.

She had an impression that was a handful too many for her dad.

Their most recent encounter was when the extended family convened for Cousin Julia's wedding back in 2014. The idea of renewing the acquaintance didn't thrill Queenie, but she knew the value of leveraging any advantage possible, and all her other attempts had failed her.

Besides, her dad had suggested it.

Shane and Liberty didn't know about their daughter's current fix because she hadn't told them.

Liberty Hart was a renowned exponent of self-help techniques, and she would have given excellent advice that Queenie would have agreed with—for anyone *not* inflicted with the Caledonian Curse.

Shane would have been troubled, and he didn't like to be troubled. He had made what provision he could afford for his only daughter. He had laid his cards on the table, and he had been more than fair. That, to him, was that.

It was this attribute of Shane Hart's personality that had led him to take her to the pub one day a few months after her eighteenth birthday for what he termed *a celebratory drink and a little dad-to-daughter heart-to-heart.*

The drink turned out to be a tiny nip of whiskey well-drowned in lemonade.

Shane downed his share neat.

Queenie Hart. January, 2016

"Cheers, love."

"Cheers, Dad. What's up?"

"Look, you're still set on moving out of home, right?"

"Yes."

She was determined to go before October brought another dose of Caledonia to her speech and another dose of annoyance from her mum.

"And you know the boomerang can't come back, right?"

"Yes, Dad. You've told me often enough."

"Fair enough. My dad told me, and his dad told him. It doesn't mean we don't love our kids."

"I know. I love you, too."

"But kids are only kids until they choose to go independent."

"Yes, and there's no becoming un-independent after you take the step."

He nodded. "Right. No boomerang. Once you leave home, you're emancipated. That doesn't mean we're kicking you out right now. You're welcome to stay on for another year or two, or three."

"No thanks. Cheyenne from work's getting a unit. She needs help with the rent, so I'm going to move in with her."

"Safe place?"

"It's one of the new units down Mother Goose Lane."

"Okay. That's a good area. Once you're moved and properly settled, your mum and I are gone—we always said we'd head off on our travels once you were independent. Right?"

"Yes." She felt a qualm. They *had* always said they'd be off travelling when she left home, but the thought of not having a home base *at all* was as frightening as it was liberating.

"So, before you make this move, think hard. I don't want you to regret it."

Queenie wavered for a moment. Still, Chey was desperate for a flatmate, and they got along well. Queenie got along with Chey's bloke, too, which was a plus. Chey was little, skinny, and dark, and her bloke loved her to bits. Queenie was definitely *not* the bloke's type.

And the idea of spending another October with her parents made her desperate to escape.

She loved them dearly, and she knew they loved her. They all got along . . . for eleven months of the year.

Shane continued, "We're giving you a lump sum to invest. It's not a fortune, but it should help with the deposit when you want to buy a place . . . let it collect interest for a bit. That's all you can depend on from us in the way of inheritance. We reckon you might as well have it now as when *we* shuffle off, which won't be for a few decades yet. No knowing what we'll be worth then, but you'll likely be middle-aged anyway."

He puffed out his cheeks.

"That's fine, Dad. You and Mum have worked hard. You deserve to enjoy yourselves."

"Yeah. I'll pick up work here and there . . ."

"I'm sure you will. A good tradie is hard to find, and you're the best."

"Okay then. There's just one thing I want to tell you. It's a bit of advice I had from my dad when I left home. Seemed odd at the time, mind, and I never needed to take it."

"Yes?"

"If you're ever in a bind that you can't get out of—look up Branok St Ives. Actually—your grandad told me to look up his dad, Mars, but it comes to the same thing."

"I thought you didn't get on."

"We don't. Never did. But there's no getting away from the fact that Bran's dad is good at finding loopholes and back doors. He's always ready to discover—or maybe to invent—a precedent. He knows all about wiggle room. And Bran's the same, on steroids."

"So—"

Shane explained briefly, and generally, what his cousin did, and for whom he did it. He didn't go into detail, but Queenie was able to mentally fill in the gaps from her eighteen years of living with parents who didn't mince their words.

"I'm not saying Bran could help you in all circumstances, but if anyone knows how to play the system and make the unfair seem fair, it's him. Whether he'd help *you,* I don't know."

"Because you don't get on?"

He gave her a sheepish grin. "To be fair, that's mostly down to me, Queenie. If I'd been a bit more tolerant when we were youngsters, maybe we'd be more civil now. I wasn't kind to him, though, in my defence, he was an arrogant little prick. You know the saying though—blood's thicker than water, and at least some of his blood's the same colour as mine."

That was all Shane had to say on the subject, and from the expression on his face he didn't think his cousin's skills—or his blood—were necessarily a good thing to investigate.

Queenie thanked him and put it out of her mind.

Wiggle room indeed. Why would I ever need wiggle room?

Queenie Hart. August, 2021

Now, years later, she was at an impasse, so perhaps it was time to put her dad's advice to the test.

With another Halloween looming in her not-too-distant future, Queenie caught a train and walked several blocks to tap on the door of Branok St Ives' city office.

No one was at Reception, so she walked round to the hutch and hit the intercom. She heard it come live.

"Branok? Are you in?"

He had never said *Call-me-Branok* on any of their infrequent meetings, but they were related, so it didn't seem appropriate to address him as *Mister St Ives.*

The door to the inner office swung open. "Who wants to know?"

Queenie's back prickled at the voice—it had the same intonation as her dad's, yet it was sharper and considerably more precise. She poked her head in. "Hello."

Branok St Ives, dark, imperious looking, and dressed in something with far too many zippers, stared at her for a few seconds before his face showed cautious recognition. "I know I should know you, but I can't place you."

His tone suggested this displeased him.

"The last time you saw me was at Julia Hennessy's wedding. I was about seventeen then. You've hardly changed, but I expect I have. We're both related to Julia, and to one another," she said.

"Then I expect you're Queenie Hart. Shane and Liberty's girl."

"That's right." She wasn't crazy about being labelled in relation to her parents, but she supposed it was fair enough, since she was leveraging the family connection.

"What a gorgeous dog. What's its name?" She'd spotted a black spaniel lounging in a luxurious dog bed near the desk. The plushness of the cushioning suggested it was an expensive bed, *ergo* the dog was indulged and valued. And that meant St Ives was attached to it.

A bit of interest taken in his pet might butter her bread, and besides, she had no objection to dogs.

Quite the reverse. Under the influence of the Caledonian Curse back in 2019, she'd almost bought a pedigreed Scottish terrier. Luckily she hadn't completed the transaction, because Angel Petty absolutely forbade pets.

"That's Lady Velvet," he said.

The dog looked up at the sound of her name. She had intelligent eyes in an odd colour.

"She's beautiful." Queenie stepped closer. She would have petted the dog, but something in those eyes made her withdraw her hand.

"How old is she?" she asked, reversing to a safe distance.

He looked startled and then he said, "It's hard to say. If we're talking human years, she might be anything from mid-thirties to late forties, depending on how you work it out."

Queenie almost said she was talking actual years, but she decided to let it alone. The dog was no pup, but she didn't look old. Presumably, Branok meant she was middle-aged.

"How may I help you, Queenie?" St Ives motioned to a chair, and she sat down. "I'm assuming this isn't a social visit. If it were, you'd have come to the house and possibly rung ahead to make sure it was convenient."

Ouch. "I don't know where you live."

"You were just passing and thought you'd pay me a cousinly visit?" His gaze sharpened, and he said in a warmer tone, "Nothing wrong with Shane, I trust? I don't act for him professionally, but I would help if he needed me to . . ."

"Nothing's wrong with Dad, so far as I know. They were both fine, last time I spoke with them."

She didn't add that this occasion had been two months before when she'd called her mother to wish her a happy birthday.

She added, "This isn't a social call, but I'm sure my parents would want me to pass on their greetings if they knew I was here."

"I'm not," he said in a dry voice. "What *do* you want?"

Queenie came to the point. She was realising exactly why Shane had never cultivated a close friendship with his cousin. Branok wasn't hostile, but he was blunt, and she was sure he didn't like folk wasting his time. He was *to-the-point,* which made him more like her dad than either man would have wanted to acknowledge.

"I need a place to live," she said.

"I'm not a real estate broker and I'm not looking for a tenant," he said.

"I know. You're a solicitor. It says so on your door."

"Then why—"

She cut in, "Dad told me you sometimes help certain people get established with property . . . and papers . . . He wasn't very specific, but he said it could be an option if I ever needed it."

He looked amused. "*Certain people*. I like that. Sounds dark and dodgy, which shows what Cousin Shane thinks of me."

"I didn't mean it to sound like that."

"I absolve you."

"Dad has never said anything—"

"I'm sure Dad *has,* but I absolve him, too. I was a tag-along trial to him when we were younger. I didn't appreciate how obnoxious I must have been until my sons hit their middle teens and turned into supercilious, know-it-all, self-entitled twits. Thank goodness they're grown and settled now." He sighed. "I would like to be on better terms with Shane, now we're so far past those days of our youth, but I've never found a way to bridge the gap."

Maybe by helping me!

But Queenie didn't really think that would help, since Shane had no idea she was in a fix.

"To return to the point . . . I do help *certain people* with establishment," he said.

"So will you help me get established in the property market? I don't want to trade or make money from it and I'm not looking for luxury. I just want a safe, secure place to live and to work."

"I'm sorry." He hesitated again and then said, "Let me try to put this delicately . . . It's not that I don't want to help you, but that I can't. You're not one of those certain people."

Queenie had expected this sort of response, but she had enough of Shane's genes to argue her corner if necessary. She looked St Ives steadily in the eye. "What do I have to do to become one of those people?"

"You can't. You don't fit the demographic."

"How do you know? Isn't there wiggle room? I mean, what *is* the demographic?"

St Ives steepled his fingers. "What do you think it is? What did your dad tell you?"

"Dad didn't say, straight out, but I'm guessing one has to be green-blooded to qualify. Is that right?"

His eyebrows flew up. "*Green-blooded!* Great bogle, what the *feck* has Shane been saying?"

"I beg your pardon. I didn't mean to be offensive."

"I should hope not, since you're asking for a favour."

"That wouldn't stop me, necessarily. I've always thought it dishonest to mince words if they're the truth. What I meant was, I didn't realise that *was* offensive. I thought it was just like—well—having a dash of the blarney if you were Irish, or being called a Kiwi if you came from—"

"I think you'd better stop right there."

"Okay. What should I say, then?"

"If you need to refer to my blood at all—and I assure you it's exactly the same colour as yours, and that no chemist has ever been able to prove it differs in any measurable—"

"Yes?"

"*If* you need to speak of my genetic make-up, you might call me a halfling, with the fay blood running at a little more than fifty-percent."

"Thank you. Then I assume you mean one has to have green—I mean *fay* blood to qualify for your help."

Branok began to nod and then froze, his eyes turning inwards.

"Yes?" she pressed.

"Normally, yes. Almost exclusively."

"How about abnormally? Unexclusively?"

"Has anyone ever told you how exasperating you are, Queenie Hart?"

"Plenty of people, repeatedly, especially Mum. But I'm desperate."

"I believe you. Up until a few years ago I'd have said a categorical *yes,* people I help this way have to be fay, and preferably full fay. However, back in twenty-seventeen I did stretch a point to help a young woman who was—as far as anyone knows—a hundred percent human."

"Why could you help her and not me?"

"She was a special case. Possibly unique."

"Why? What made her special if I'm not?"

St Ives turned the full force of his annoyance on her. "I'm not telling you her history or her business. I'm bound by client confidentiality as well as morality. I *do* have a moral code, despite what Shane might have implied. I like to be able to look myself in the eye when I'm shaving. And *yes,* I do shave with a razor. I don't apply—er—weedkiller. And *yes,* I can handle iron with no worse consequences than you."

Queenie bit her lip.

"Although admittedly I might not shave as often as full humans. It's rare to find a fay man with a beard—unless he's—oh—*bleddy hell—*"

Queenie startled herself, and him, with a giggle.

St Ives sighed and then he said, "Since you're obviously going to persist until I throw you out of my office, I'll tell you this much—the young woman in question is human, but she spent a great deal of her life *over there.* Do you know what I mean by that? And please don't say *Greenland.*"

"Fairyland," she said.

"If you like, though *we* certainly don't call it that. Have you ever been *over there*?"

She shook her head. "Have you?"

"Yes, often. I have cousins up at Treborrow, and my wife's parents have retired not far from there. I was born on this side of the gates, and so were my dad and *his* dad, but we've always maintained close ties with family *over there.*

"Anyhow, when my client returned to the human realm, she wanted to resume an identity she'd used for a two-year stretch ending in two-thousand-and-nine. She had no accessible relatives, no friends, no home, no savings, and no income. She quite literally had nothing but her clothes, a fiddle, and a couple of bags."

"I see. Poor girl." Queenie felt it necessary to say that, although as far as she could see she wasn't in a much better case. She had her identity, but what good had that ever done her? "Is she okay now?"

"Yes. I was privileged to stand in as her surrogate father at her wedding." He went on staring at her. "I can't say I know much about you, Queenie, but from what I know of your dad and mum, you would have had a decent education, and you probably have fair intelligence and good health. You certainly have good looks and probably a good deal of personal charm when you're not being exasperating. Shane and Liberty did a good job by you. You don't twitch or blink excessively and you don't smell of anything unfortunate. Your clothing is clean, and you have all your teeth."

"Please—stop."

He nodded. "I will then. And yes, perhaps I *was* being offensive. I'm assuming your parents haven't disowned you. You haven't done anything they'd think was reprehensible or beyond the human pale?"

"Nothing like that. We're not estranged, but I can't live with them or apply to them for funds for a house. For one thing, they made the anti-boomerang clause clear to me years ago. Even if they hadn't, they sold up and turned into grey nomads a few months after I left home. Not that they're grey . . . Dad took early retirement, and he picks up building jobs wherever he is. Mum can do what she does anywhere."

Mum was Liberty Hart, of *Harts Ease* and *Liberate Your Hart* self-help fame, but Queenie didn't feel it necessary to inform him of something he must already know.

Branok St Ives nodded his comprehension. "I believe my mother did mention they were no longer at the old address when she was sending Christmas letters, but I hadn't realised they'd gone right away. They have no property at all in Sydney?"

"None anywhere, as far as I know. They have a mobile home, a small runabout, and bikes."

"Where are you living currently?"

She explained about the unit and the truculent landlady.

"Why did you move in there if it's so oppressive?"

"I moved in with a friend from the job I had then. She needed help with the rent. It was fine for a while. Chey dealt with tenant stuff. After a while, I lost that job, and after I got another one, Chey decided to move in with her boyfriend. Ms Petty—the landlady—let me take over the lease, but she wasn't pleased. It turned out she'd given Chey a good rate because she's some sort of relative, and she's not keen to have me there at the same rate. Since I started Queen of Tarts—my little baking business—she's even less pleased. She's been making life difficult in all sorts of little ways." She sighed. "To be fair, she's technically in the right about the zoning laws. She's given me an ultimatum. Either I give up my little business—at least on her premises—or else I have to leave at the end of the year when Chey's initial agreement runs out."

"Awkward."

"I have some capital. Mum and Dad gave me a lump sum when they sold the house. It was supposed to earn good interest in a term deposit, and I was able to roll the interest over for the first couple of terms. Interest levels have flatlined now and I'm just barely keeping afloat. I need a property I can afford . . .somewhere I can work and live . . . and I need it before the beginning of October."

"I thought you had until the end of the year?"

"Not exactly."

"Then I suggest you jump on some real estate sites or answer advertisements for a flatmate as a matter of priority."

He sounded dismissive, and that made Queenie angry. "Do you think I haven't done that already? I've been doing that since Chey left, and lately I've lowered my sights and looked for *anything*. There's *nothing* I can afford, and I'm not keen to have my little nest egg eaten up in rent. I'm looking for a fair go, not for a free ride."

"That's good, because there's no such thing."

"Some people get rides denied to other people."

"People who work the system, you mean."

"It's not only that. Mum's a writer. Lots of writers apply for grants, and that's how they support themselves. Mum looked into that before they sold up. She said there were lots of grants she can't apply for, because she's too old, too young, too experienced, writes in the wrong genre, lives in the wrong place, or is the wrong ethnicity." She took a deep breath. "How did you help the person you told me about? I mean, what exactly did you do for her?"

"I recommended her for an inheritance property. And before you ask, I'm afraid you don't qualify for that level of help. You're not fay—"

"Neither is she . . . right?" She paused for a few seconds, and then she delivered what she hoped was a facer. "Besides, I do have some green blood—I beg your pardon—fay ancestry."

St Ives failed to look as stunned as she hoped and expected.

"I really do. I'm not making it up. Mum told me, and it's not the sort of thing she'd say if it wasn't true."

He gave her an odd smile. "Well now—I believe you, though I didn't know until you mentioned it. It must be through Liberty, because Shane hasn't any. I get my fay blood from both my parents, but Shane is related to the human half of my mother's family."

"Does Mum's blood qualify me?"

He shook his head. "I'm sorry, but no. A large percentage of the population has a trace of fay blood, even though the majority don't know it or don't know how it fits in their family tree. But even if you were one hundred percent proof pixie or elf or leppy, which you can't possibly be, you still wouldn't qualify for a property."

"Why not?" She wondered if he was making up the rules—or changing them—as he went along.

"Because you, like me and my sons . . . and my wife, for that matter—were born in the human realm. You've always lived here. You've never been *over there* to visit, let alone spent years living there. You're not displaced. This is your home. You're an Australian citizen by right of birth.

"The people I occasionally help out are the ones who come *over here* as sponsored young adults and who decide they want to settle and *live human* as we put it. And it's only a small percentage of those. Most of them have friends or relatives to provide them with a home base until they get on their feet or change their minds. If they have no history here, and no near relatives or friends, I put them in touch with the inheritance fund and help them to acquire starter papers. That puts them on a more even footing with their peers who were born here. It lets them exist in the human system. It's a one-shot deal, though."

"They'd be on a better footing than mine," she sniped. "Considering they have a choice, and I haven't. They could always just stay where they were born. They're not refugees or anything . . . are they? They just come over for—oh, I don't know—" She stopped short. She'd been going to say *for the chance to lord it over mere humans,* but that was obviously a bad idea.

"You might choose to look at it that way. But you may be sure that even with the limited help I provide, they still have to work hard to establish themselves. They can't just walk into a job or a fortune. They have to learn to conform with the human way—or at least to appear to. They have to work and contribute to society . . . and in my experience a lot of them work a damned sight harder than the human born. They *want* to work here . . . they don't *have* to.

"All I do is to ensure they don't have to start with nothing but the clothes they were wearing when they came through."

"I see," Queenie said.

She smiled and stood up. "Well, thank you for explaining, Branok."

"You're leaving?" St Ives sounded startled.

"It's obvious you're not going to help me. And before you start explaining *again,* I quite see why you won't. I didn't understand how it worked. Now I do. I honestly thought Mum's green—*fay* blood would give me a footing."

"I'm sorry."

"That's okay. It was worth a try. Back to the drawing board."

Chapter Seven: Manifestation

Queenie Hart. August, 2021

Branok St Ives nodded, his glance straying to some paperwork he'd evidently been attending to before she came in. Then he said, unexpectedly, "Why do you have to move *now*? Or, as you put it, before October? Have you actually been evicted?"

"No, although I'm on thin ice with my landlady. It's because of the Caledonian Curse."

He pushed the papers away. "What's that?"

"I don't know *what* it is. I just know the effect it has." She put her hand on the door.

Branok St Ives laughed. "I'm not letting you leave without explaining that. Curiosity is my overweening trait, as my wife will tell you. Come through to the sitting room and I'll get Gill to organise some lunch."

"You said you can't help me."

"I know I did, but that doesn't mean I can't give my kissing cousin some lunch. Don't worry. It won't be ambrosia or honeydew, and you won't be doomed to live with the demon king for six months of the year."

He got up and opened a door that Queenie hadn't noticed before. He beckoned her through to a comfortable room with a small kitchen built in.

She sat down while he went to switch the kettle on. When it boiled, he poured three cups of tea, brought them to the table, and settled opposite her.

The door they'd just come through opened, and a tall woman in dark blue jeans and a royal blue blouse came in, carrying a covered tray. She wore a lot of silver jewellery, and Queenie identified her as Branok's wife Gillan, whom she'd last seen at Julia's wedding.

Gillan nodded affably to her. "Hello again, Queenie." She laid out sandwiches and slices of cake on the low table. Then she sat down next to her husband and waited expectantly.

Queenie, puzzled by her presence and her immediate recognition of someone she surely hadn't expected to see, accepted a sandwich.

"Tell us about the Caledonian Curse," Branok said.

Queenie told them. "So you see, I have to move before October, because there's a good chance I'll accidentally spend my nest egg on a Scottie dog, or a genuine cairngorm, or maybe a week in a Scottish castle," she ended.

When she finished, Branok leaned back and glanced at his wife. "That's one of the odder tales I've heard this year. Have you ever heard of anything as mad as that, Gill?"

"It's absolutely true," Queenie said.

"I don't doubt it. It's too bizarre not to be true."

"Sounds like a manifestation," Gillan said. She added, inconsequentially, "By the way, I'd avoid the Scottie dog if I were you. We lived with one for several years, so we're in a position to know."

Branok said, "Could be a mani. One of the seasonal type."

"What's a manifestation? Some sort of haunting? Or possession? Are you saying I have a fecking ghost in my head?" Queenie asked.

"Not a ghost," Gillan said.

"No such thing," her husband added.

"What then? A Halloween ghoulie?"

They shook their heads.

"Jack O'Lantern?"

"Now you're just being silly," Gillan said dampeningly.

"Then what? Some ancient Scottish witch?"

"No such thing as those, either," Branok said. "Probably not even a bogle." He held up his hand, forestalling her next suggestion. "It's quite impossible to explain properly because no one knows exactly what they are, but if it is a manifestation, it *won't* do you any harm. It's not anything bad."

"Annoying and inconvenient, maybe," Gillan put it.

"They can be embarrassing," Branok said.

"But not, repeat, *not* harmful," Gillan stressed with a quelling look at her husband. "Not in women, anyway."

"It nearly did me a lot of harm last time," Queenie objected. She told them about the almost-purchased round-trip ticket to Scotland. "So you see, Scottie dogs and bottles of scotch and lucky heather are not the half of it. I had a personal bagpipe serenade one year. It cost me over three hundred dollars. The landlady had a conniption and my neighbour thought I'd gone mad. To cap it off, I tried to seduce the piper."

Gillan failed to hide amusement.

"It's not funny. I was mortified. I can't afford to blow my little nest egg on non-refundable tickets *or* Scottish castles, or in paying fines for harassing Scotsmen, but nor can I afford to have it tied up in cast-iron term deposits when I have no income for the month."

"No-o, but I'd *love* to know what would have happened if you'd actually gone to Scotland . . . or run off with the piper."

"I'll never know, because I'll never go," she said.

"Oh, I don't know . . . you could always go via—"

Branok shook his head at Gillian.

"Is there any way to get this manifestation out of me?" Queenie asked.

"I suppose a hypnotist or someone who uses influence—one of our sons, for example—might be able to suppress it, but it would still be there," Gillan said.

Queenie shuddered. "Ugh."

"It's not a bad thing," Branok repeated.

"All very well for you to say. You don't have a creepy *thing* in your head trying to take over your life at Halloween."

"And neither do you," Gillan said. "It's not a *thing.* It's a part of you, expressing itself seasonally."

"Have you talked to your parents about this?" Branok asked.

"Not lately. It didn't start till I was in my teens, and they used to get cranky with me because they thought I was doing it on purpose. I remember Dad saying if I *had* to put on a stage accent, I might at least get it right."

She saw Branok and his wife exchange a fleeting glance. She was sure they were communicating at some level.

Gillan caught her gaze. "We've been assuming this is a manifestation because it seems the most plausible explanation, but it's just struck me that in your case it *isn't* plausible. Just where do you fit in the family tree, Queenie?"

Queenie frowned. "I think Branok and Dad are second cousins . . . or is it first cousins once removed?"

"That wasn't what I meant."

"She meant, which common ancestor do we share," Branok put in. "I can answer that, Gill. Shane comes from Ma-Ma's mother's line—the Enderbys. I think our maternal great-grandmothers were sisters."

"She's from the human side of the bed, then," Gillan said.

"Yes."

Gillan turned to Queenie. "And yet you said you have some fay ancestry?"

"Yes. It was someone on Mum's side, but I don't know exactly who, and neither does she. It must be a long way back. She remembers Gran saying an old lady—someone she called *Auntie Violet*—told her she had fairy blood, but she's not sure who she was. Gran called some of her parents' and grandparents' friends *Auntie* and *Uncle* whether they were related to her or not. I couldn't believe Mum never followed it up, but she said apparently Auntie Violet was the only one who mentioned it, and by the time she tried to get the details everyone who might have known was either dead or too old to remember."

"That puts the manifestation back on the table," Branok said.

"It shouldn't. Once you get back to trace fay . . . I've never heard of a mani in *anyone* who was less than a quarterling, and even if Liberty had one full fay parent, Queenie would still *be* a quarterling."

"Maybe she is."

"Surely not. Liberty *would* know if she was a halfling, even if no one told her, because she'd most likely be able to do things her peers couldn't—"

Queenie felt excluded and ignored as they argued the point. She drained her tea and, for the second time, rose to her feet to leave.

Branok held out a hand to detain her. "Queenie, I don't think we're going to get to the bottom of this if Liberty really doesn't know, and I won't pretend to know exactly what's going on with you, but I think maybe you're qualified for my help after all."

"I *am*?" Cautious hope flared, and she sat down.

"The fund helps young folk whose fay blood and upbringing puts them at a grave disadvantage in the human realm. *Your* fay blood, wherever it originates, is putting you at a disadvantage." He sounded as if he were trying to convince himself.

"Am I right in supposing you find it difficult to hold down a normal nine-to-five job?"

She nodded. "I have tried asking for October off, but because I was low on the pecking order it was *request denied.*"

"And then when you started channelling the Caledonian Curse at work, I assume it got you into trouble."

"It got me sacked, because I called my supervisor a scabby scrote and told her that her bum was out the windae. I don't even know what that means! It's also got me psychoanalysed when I was at school when I lit into a bully and told her that her maw's git baws . . . I don't know which is worse, getting sacked or getting psyched. These days, I get by on casual and part-time work and my own small baking business. I'm hoping to expand that as soon as I have the room and the time. But it's a bit of the chicken and the egg. Because I can't work full time, I can't qualify for home loans, and because I need to work from home, I can't stay in my current unit, even if I wanted to."

Again, the St Ives couple exchanged a look.

Branok said, "I think it would be fair to say Queenie qualifies . . . just. What do you think? I'm not being partial?"

His wife eyed him with amusement. "Considering you couldn't put a name to the face when she turned up, and then you gave her the run-around . . . And considering you don't need, or want, your cousin's or your cousin's wife's good opinion . . . I think it's safe to say you're being impartial where their daughter is concerned."

"Good. I hoped so. It's a mistake to indulge in reverse nepotism." He got up and went to a filing cabinet.

Gillan caught Queenie's eye and gave her a small but definite wink.

Branok came back and held out a slip of paper. "Queenie, here's a number to call. It will put you through to the offices of the Porthwellian Tredennick Inheritance Fund. Ask to speak with Andy Tredennick. I can't say whether he'll approve you, as he's a junior partner, but he's the one most likely to give you a sympathetic hearing. He may have to pass you up the food chain, but you can tell him I recommended you as a possible fit for a property called The Belfry."

"Really?" Gillan sounded startled.

"It's the best I can do for her. She's marginally qualified, and The Belfry is marginally suitable."

Queenie took the number. She felt stunned. "Th-thank you *so* much." Her voice shook.

"Don't thank me yet. You may not be approved, and even if you are, you might not find the property suitable."

"Why wouldn't I?"

Gillan said, "Other people haven't. It's got a bit of a reputation."

"Why?"

But Gillan refused to say.

"If you're approved, and if you decide to view the property, I suggest you take it on a short-term lease first," Branok said. He sounded as if he were regretting his offer.

Queenie nodded, and, clutching the precious telephone number, she left the office before he could talk himself out of it.

Once she was on the train, she carefully stored the number in her phone and tucked the paper into her purse to be on the safe side.

She was halfway back to her unit before it occurred to her to wonder how Gillan had known she had distant fay ancestry. Branok hadn't known until she told him. Nor should Gillan have known he hadn't immediately recognised her, or that they needed lunch. Had Gillan been hiding in a cupboard or behind another unnoticeable door? Surveillance cameras? One-way windows? Or did she simply have super hearing? Her parents lived in Fairyland . . .

Chapter Eight: Porthwellian Tredennick

Queenie Hart. August, 2021

It was already the middle of August, so Queenie had no time to waste. She called the number as soon as she was back in Mother Goose Lane.

She half expected it to ring out, but after three rings a male voice answered.

"Porthwellian Tredennick. Androw Tredennick speaking. How may I direct your call?"

"Andy Tredennick?"

"Speaking," he said patiently. He had a pleasant voice that sounded as if he were on the verge of smiling.

Having mentally prepared to be not answered, put on hold, or caught in an endless loop of re-direction, Queenie let the silence stretch for quite five seconds.

"Hello?"

She said, "I wasn't expecting *you* to answer. I thought it would be an assistant or a robo-phone."

"We get that a lot," he said.

"Okay. Yes. My name is Queenie Hart." She spelled it for him. "I went to see Branok St Ives today, and he gave me your number. He suggested I might qualify to rent a property called The Belfry."

"We do have a property of that name on our books." He sounded so pleased he might have been congratulating her on winning the lottery.

"He said I should ask about a short-term lease."

"That's probably wise. Properties and people need to *fit*. Do you want to view it now?"

"Well—yes. If I—that is—where is it, exactly?"

If he was surprised that someone would enquire about a property without knowing where it was, he didn't betray it. He said, "It's just north of Fiddle Bay. That's in New South Wales. Where are you calling from?"

"Sydney," she said.

"Well, then, you probably know the area. "

"I know the town, yes—I mean, I've been through it occasionally. When can I see it?"

"Soon as you like," he said.

Too easy. Much too easy.

He went on, "I need some details from you first."

Definitely, *much too easy*. Here came the catch.

She waited to be told she must download a form from a website with an incomprehensible address full of dots and back-slashes and fill it out with information she didn't have to hand and sign it electronically and then have it refuse to execute.

Instead, Tredennick said, "Full name?"

She told him.

"Current address, or proxy address where you can receive mail?"

She hesitated and then she gave him Branok St Ives' office. The situation with the landlady might go critical at any moment.

"Is the best phone number the one you're calling from?"

"Yes."

"Email?"

"Queenoftarts at jamandbutter dot com." She spelled it out.

"Date of birth?"

She gave it.

"Qualification for applying to the fund?"

For the first time Queenie had to choose her words with care. If she stuffed this up, friendly Andy Tredennick might say she didn't qualify after all, and he was sorry, but . . .

"I have a problem that means I can't work or function socially in October, especially near the end. Branok and his wife said they think it's a *manifestation,*" she said, aware of how ridiculous it sounded.

"Ah! A seasonal Halloween mani! It's been decades since we've had one of those to deal with. *So* rare! Christmas manis are two-a-penny, but *Halloween!*" He sounded *pleased.*

"Are you old enough to remember back that far?" she asked.

"I'm twenty-six, so no, I don't remember, but I like to keep abreast of the records," he said. The was a slight pause and she heard the tapping of keys. "Okay, Mistress Hart—"

"*Mistress*?"

"Not?"

She realised what he might mean. "I forgot to mention, I'm human—mostly. Is that an impediment?"

"Generally it would be, but in your case, you come in under the special circumstances clause. If you have a mani, there had to be a fairy in the bed at some point in your recent genetic past." He laughed. "Don't worry, Mistress . . . Ms Hart. Would you like us to send the keys, or would you prefer someone to come through and show you around the property?"

Startled, she said nothing.

"Ms Hart?"

"Ah—whichever is easier," she managed. "It would be nice if you—"

"It would take me a couple of hours . . ." She heard him humming tunelessly. "No, the tide's high. Make that six or seven hours before I could be with you. It would be much faster to have Oliver send the keys directly to The Belfry. Do you have something to write down the address, or shall I text it to you?"

"B-both," she stammered. "Please."

"Okay. The property name is The Belfry. The address is Thirty-One October Road, Kirk Circle, just north of Fiddle Bay. Drive out of town, heading north, and the turn-off is on the right, about two kilometres past the *Leaving Fiddle Bay* sign. Think you can find it?"

"Yes," she said faintly. She didn't mention that she didn't have a car.

"Good. I'll text you the directions when I hang up. The key will be—" He paused, and she heard someone else speak briefly in the background. He continued, "Pegged to the clothesline in the garden. Look about . . . stay a couple of days if you want. Oliver says he'll organise a few basic groceries, but no bedding or fresh stuff. Still, you're not far out of town. Turn the power on at the meter box just inside the big door. Okay?"

"Yes, but—"

"Oliver won't do that. He doesn't hold with meters. When and if you decide the place is a good fit for you, give us another bell. If not, lock up, put the key back where you got it, and let us know."

The line went dead.

Queenie looked at her phone in disbelief.

Someone knocked on the door and opened it without waiting for an answer.

Startled, Queenie looked into the cold brown eyes of her landlady.

"Inspection."

"I've only just got home and I'm on my way out again," Queenie said.

The woman stepped forward. So did Queenie.

"You're meant to give me written notice before an inspection. It's not convenient."

"It's convenient for me." The landlady's face had a truculent look.

Queenie closed the door, obliging the woman to step back.

She just couldn't deal with Angel Petty today.

Anyone less like an angel . . . but she is *petty.*

She had intended to have a late lunch before venturing out again, but she'd had sandwiches with the St Ives couple. Was that only an hour ago?

She went to the old wooden chest that did duty as a wardrobe and took out some clean underwear and a jacket, her camp pillow, and her sleeping bag. She changed into sensible shoes and headed back towards the train station.

"Ms Hart! A word!" Ms Petty called as she left.

"Later. I told you, I'm going out."

She caught the train just in time and sat down in a daze of confusion.

Ms Petty would be pissed. As in seriously pissed. As in giving her notice pissed.

That should have put the fear of Magog into her, but she was on her way to view a property.

It couldn't possibly be this easy.

Chapter Nine: The Belfry

Queenie Hart. August, 2021

Andy Tredennick had assumed she'd be driving herself, but Queenie caught a train to Borrowdale Junction. From there, she transferred to a green-painted minibus which took her right through Fiddle Bay.

There was a small hiccup when her three-six-five announced it was "out of zone" and she had to find cash for the bus driver, but aside from a couple of indignant looks from other passengers at the delay it was okay.

Fiddle Bay was a coastal town, with houses and cottages following the sweep of the long curving cove that gave the settlement its name. It spread a few streets inland, but the bus followed what she supposed was called an esplanade, stopping near the post office for passengers to alight. It was evidently a local service because most of them thanked the driver by name.

"Thanks, Mitch."

"See you later, Mitch."

He answered them with a friendly quip or comment and got out to assist a woman with a stroller and an elderly man with a walker.

"Excuse me, but where's the next stop?" Queenie asked as he stepped back up into the bus after disembarking the man.

"Up at the big house," he said, settling back into his seat.

"That's not much help."

"What?" He glanced over his shoulder and stared at her for

a few seconds. "Sorry. I thought you were a local. The big house is the common name for Oakengrove. That's—"

"Is that the place that holds the concerts?"

"Yes—if you're talking about the *Oakengrove Experience.* It happens late next month. I can take you—"

"Where's the next stop after that, today?"

"That's the end of the road for this run. The bigger services go up and down the coast, but this is the Borrowdale Junction—Oakengrove Express. So to speak. Where did you want to go?" He turned away, pushed his over-large cap back from his eyes and put the bus in gear.

"A place called The Belfry."

"That's a couple of kay outside of town, beyond the big house."

"I know. Is there a car hire place here?"

He raised his voice above the engine as the bus whirred away from the post office. "Not in the bay, and the one in Borrow is only open sometimes. I can run you out to the circle if you like, but I have pick-ups at the big house going back to the station. Time's tight. I'm afraid I can't wait long for you."

"I don't need you to wait," she said.

She didn't elaborate, because it occurred to her that telling a stranger she was fetching a key from a clothesline and potentially staying the night in a strange house might not be a good idea.

How the hell was Andy Tredennick sending the key, anyway? It couldn't be permanently hung from a clothesline.

He'd said something about the tide, and something about Oliver, but how were they relevant?

She shrugged. What was the worst that could happen? The key wouldn't be there, and she'd have to walk back into town carrying her pack or try calling the number again for further instructions.

She wouldn't mind another conversation with Andy

Tredennick. He was friendly, and helpful, and he seemed to actively want her to have what she needed.

It came to her that it was a *very* long time since someone had been squarely in her corner.

She remembered the living statue she'd seen at Circular Quay the year before. *He* had given her a wish. She had used it for him.

Yes, and almost directly after that I met lovely James Stuart and then it all went to pot.

The bus made quick work of the trip to the turn-off.

"October Road," the driver said over his shoulder. "I can take you to the circle and then turn round and you can get off. If you're sure you want to. There's nothing much out here."

Queenie peered out of the window. They had left the coast, and all around was open grassland and some trees dotted about. If she was going to Number Thirty-One, where were numbers one to thirty?

The bus slowed at a circular drive outside a low stone wall. An arched gateway bore the sign *October Road Graveyard.*

"This can't be the right place," Queenie said as the bus finished its turn and paused.

"The Belfry's over there," the driver said, indicating some tall and no doubt ancient trees. "Do you need a hand down? I'd be happy to help you."

"Oh, no . . . thanks." Queenie, feeling oddly reluctant, got up and hoisted her pack over one shoulder. She moved forward and clambered down the two steep steps and made the last long stride to the gravel. No wonder the old man and the woman with the stroller had needed assistance.

"Thanks . . . um . . . Mitch," she said. She smelled the sudden faint tang of eucalyptus. Polish? Or was it one of those dangling tree-shaped deodorisers?

"No worries," he said easily. "Are you staying around these parts for long?"

"I don't know."

The door sighed closed. The bus departed.

Queenie stood by the graveyard gate and stared after the retreating vehicle.

What kind of bus driver goes out of his way to take someone out of town?

Then she turned to survey the dark trees halfway around the wall.

It was a short walk, and she was aware of the silence. A crow—or was it a raven—cawed at her in a snide *warrk, warrk, warrk.*

October Road ended here, and as far as she could see, there were no other buildings. How this one could be number Thirty-One was beyond her. The numbers couldn't begin in the town, because this was a side road with a different name and B-code. Or was it a C? She couldn't recall.

She walked on, under the trees that met overhead, and came to a stop outside another low wall, or possibly a continuation of the first one.

October Road Old Rectory, she read. The sign was incised in the stone. She saw the garden ahead, but where a house might have been, there was a roughly cleared block. A few gnarled fruit trees were just starting into blossom, and sweeps of self-sufficient paperwhites, snowflakes, and daffodils brightened the grass. A trio of Japanese camellia in red, pink, and white hoisted bright flowers like flags to celebrate survival.

"What the hell?"

She got out her phone. She planned to give someone an earful, but should she call Andy Tredennick or Cousin Branok?

Wait—*property* was the word they'd both used. No one had said *house.* Nonsense. There had to be a door, because the meter box was behind one. There had to be a clothesline, and she couldn't see one yet.

There was no signal, so she walked on away from the trees and came to a sudden stop as another garden materialised around a curve in the wall. This one was also overgrown with more scruffy old trees and winter-flowering bulbs blooming under their own recognisance, but the building was intact.

Queenie felt her eyes bug. Now she knew why the property was called *The Belfry*. It was . . . or had once been . . . a church.

She hit *recall* on her phone, hardly caring who she was ringing.

"Porthwellian Tredennick, Androw Tredenn—"

"This place is a fricking church."

"So? The name might have suggested that, Ms Hart."

"You must have known."

"Ms Hart, the inheritance trust administers a lot of properties. I haven't inspected them all."

"Why not? Isn't it your duty not to send people on wild goose chases?"

He said, reproachfully, "I'm in south-eastern Victoria, you know. The senior partner, Oliver Porthwellian, knows The Belfry well, so it was he who sent the key."

"Can I speak to him, then?"

"I'm afraid not. He's gone off on his constitutional with the boys."

"Surely he has a mobile."

"He doesn't hold with them."

"Why not?"

"He's ninety-six, and they don't work where he's gone. What's the trouble? Is the key not there?"

"I haven't looked yet."

"Then I suggest you get it and let yourself in. Spend some time to get a feel for the place, then let us know if you think it will suit you."

"I forgot to ask the rent." She felt sheepish. Andy had been nice to her. Being snippy was a poor repayment. Besides . . . she needed to butter her bread. "I'm sorry for being cranky," she said.

There was a disconcerted pause.

"Mister Tredennick?"

He said, "Not to worry. I assumed Master St Ives would have explained all that. You did say he recommended the place to you."

"Yes. Never mind. I'll have a look about while I'm here, but would you text me the lease details anyway?"

"Okay." He hung up. Or maybe the call fell out.

Queenie dropped the phone in her top pocket.

The clothesline was near the door, which probably led into the vestry. It was a 1960s rotary hoist bearing a dozen or so weathered wooden pegs. The one holding the key was close to one of the arms, so the key was hidden from the casual glance.

Clever.

Queenie unclipped it and went to examine the church. It was made of Sydney sandstone, with a slate roof. A built-out area to one side with a small door suggested it might be a vestry, and a modest round belltower, topped with a mossy cross, rose to mingle with the nearest dark tree. Three dark birds perched on the cross, peering down at her with cold eyes.

The main door was up three steps and led directly into the foyer, with the belltower on the right.

Queenie climbed the steps slowly and inserted the key in the lock. A polished brass nameplate was screwed into the weathered wood.

The Belfry.

Chapter Ten: Video Call

The key turned easily, and the door opened without a creak. Queenie stepped into darkness. After a few seconds her eyes adjusted to reveal a small foyer, with standing room for possibly four parishioners and a vicar. To her right was a closed door with a heavy rope handle which looked as if it must lead up into the belltower.

She reached out and gave it a cursory tug.

Nothing happened.

Straight ahead, an open arch led into the body of the building. To her left was a square box on the wall at shoulder height. Beside that a painted arrow informed her it was the meter box.

She opened it and examined the array of switches in the dim light. One large one had *Master Switch* written under it in black marker.

Queenie moved it to the *on* position. Overhead, a warm yellow light flickered and glowed.

Whoever locked up last must have left the light on and simply turned off the power.

She walked through the arch, expecting dusty pews, a pulpit, and maybe a covered font, but instead she saw a large living area with a polished wood floor softened by a carpet square. There were two low couches and a small round table with two chairs.

The area she had thought was the vestry had been converted to a neat bathroom with tub, shower, loo, and basin. Generous bench space suggested it had originally been used for arranging and deconstructing floral tributes.

A large folding screen divided the main rectangle of the building in two, and beyond that a bedroom hovered on a mezzanine floor which might once have housed the pulpit and choir stalls. The only other room was a large and unexpectedly modern kitchen which occupied the part beyond the screen.

Queenie stepped through and found the fridge humming greedily as it sucked in power and cooled. The industrial-sized sink was dry and clean, and the bench was polished granite. A built-in pantry revealed the promised basic supplies . . . long-life milk, a sealed box of assorted crackers, tea and coffee, dry cereal, and sealed dried fruit and nuts. There was even, improbably, a slab of dark cake wrapped in greaseproof paper inside a tea towel. An electric jug balanced upside down on the edge of the sink.

"Oh!" The exclamation seemed inadequate, so Queenie said it again. "*Oh!*" She upended the kettle, rinsed and filled it, and set it to boil. She rinsed a china mug decorated with a dark, lacy pattern that might have been leaves. Then she walked up the shallow steps to the bedroom.

As she'd been warned, there was no bedding, but the bedframe was draped in a holland dust cover. Queenie pulled it off and sat down. The mattress was oddly springy, and it gave off a faint scent like dry hay. She fetched her sleeping bag from the foyer, unrolled it, and set up her pillow.

Then she returned to the kitchen, running her hands over the cool granite and opening and closing drawers and cupboards. These held basic utensils such as a can opener, plain cutlery, a marble rolling pin, and some well-used loaf tins and saucepans. There was an old-fashioned drop-side toaster with its cord wrapped neatly around it, the way a cat wraps its tail around its feet, and cups, plates and bowls bearing the same pattern as the mug.

A tilt door opened to show a bin probably meant for potatoes and onions, and its twin had traces of bran in the bottom. On the small scrubbed pine table in the kitchen stood a bottle of Scotch whiskey . . .Islay Rock single malt. A label around the neck said *Porthwellian Tredennick. Welcome to The Belfry.*

Queenie poured herself a small measure and went to sit in the main room, first removing the holland cover from a couch. As with the rest of the furnishings, it was in excellent near-new condition. It appeared to Queenie that the place had been renovated, or possibly remodelled, quite recently.

So, why don't people stay here? It's perfect!

The Belfry looked like a colonial-era church on the outside, but inside it was a gem of a studio flat with each room maximising space for the important things.

That kitchen!

Her phone pinged, announcing a text message.

Details as requested.

Greetings, Ms Hart. Here is the info you requested. Let me know if you need anything more.

A. Tredennick.

Property Name – The Belfry

Thirty-One October Road,

Kirk Circle, Nr. Fiddle Bay.

Status – available to approved applicant

In the gift of Porthwellian Tredennick

Sponsor of current applicant – Branok St Ives, solicitor and trustee

Time period – available now. Three days consideration hold. Thereafter, three months minimum, renewable upon application.

Lease – three months nil owing. Upon extension, peppercorn rent or payment in kind may be negotiated with trustees.

Utilities beyond three-day hold period to be paid by approved lessee.

Queenie's eyes blurred and she blinked several times and read it over again. If she understood the terse information which she had—*in writing* if you please—she could stay for three days and then move into this property for up to three months . . . no, for a *minimum* of three months, and live there rent free, paying only for electricity, water, and whatever else came under the heading of *utilities.* After that, she could apply to stay on, paying a negotiated rent. *Peppercorn* meant small, or nominal, and although she was aware her idea of *nominal* might not match that of the trust holders, there was always the *in-kind* payment. She wondered what that meant. Maybe she would be expected to make and maintain a garden or . . . or something.

It sounded shady, but she clung to the idea that as her dad's cousin, even if they didn't get along, Branok wouldn't steer her wrong on purpose.

What had he said?

Ah, he liked to be able to look himself in the eye when shaving. Branok St Ives might well know the loopholes and the back doors and shortcuts, but he respected his clients' privacy, and he loved his dog . . . and his wife.

Queenie was uneasily aware that it suited her purpose to believe her odd relative was on the side of the angels. She was at least certain he was on the side of the fairies . . . he *was* a fairy, although she couldn't remember Shane explicitly saying so. She had no idea what kind, but it occurred to her that if Branok was a fairy, or at least a half fairy, since he'd mentioned a percentage of fay blood, then that might explain why her dad had never been close to him. Branok was younger—a tagalong, in his own terms—so how might a wholly human teenager, prone to all the bewildering spots and spurts and turmoil of adolescence, have felt if he had a younger cousin who sailed through the whole to-do and popped up smelling like a rose?

She considered her mixed feelings when, at seventeen, she had encountered Gillan, Branok, and their sons at Julia's wedding. Gillan, so effortlessly handsome and elegant, had put the usually stylish Liberty Hart in the shade. Those boys, clear-skinned, clear-eyed, with silky dark hair that had obviously never hung limp, lank or greasy . . . no wonder they hadn't thought much of Queenie. She recalled their assessing gaze which lasted all of five seconds before they discounted her. They were younger than her, but so much more self-assured. She wasn't sure if they'd despised her, or simply deemed her beneath their notice.

They were fairy men—or at least they would be. To them, she was just a human.

I wonder if Dad knows *he resents Branok, not for being an obnoxious younger cousin, but for being what he can't ever be himself . . .*

She thought he probably didn't. Her father wasn't a mean or petty or resentful man. He wasn't given to self-examination. He was four-square and transparent as glass.

"What you see is what you get," was the way he described himself, or—"What it says on the tin."

And yet, he married Mum, and she *has some fay ancestry.*

She tried to recall exactly what she'd been told about that, but it was too long ago. As far as she remembered, it had been when the child Queenie had been enquiring her way along the byways of fairies, angels, monsters, and scary things under the bed. Her mum had told her what *old Auntie Violet* had told Gran . . . but she hadn't been able to identify Auntie Violet in the family tree.

Queenie raised her glass with the last drop of amber scotch. "*Slàinte Mhath,*" she announced, and she drained the drop and let it roll over her tongue.

Maybe toasting in a church was frowned upon, but this church could no longer be considered a *church,* exactly. It must have been unsanctified or deconsecrated, or whatever the term was, before it was turned into a studio flat.

She set the glass down and looked about with a proprietary interest.

This could be home . . . at least for three months.

At the very least she could save three months' rent . . . well over five thousand dollars.

Her spirits rose in incredulous hope.

That kitchen . . . she could afford to bake in bulk, and—

Her thoughts broke off as she remembered zoning laws. Her landlady objected to the running of her tiny baking business from her unit, on the grounds that she was using a residential area for commercial purposes.

But Mum writes her self-help stuff in residential zones . . . or she did that before they sold up. No one ever said she couldn't.

Better make sure.

Once more, she called the offices of Porthwellian Tredennick. And this time, she made it a video call.

"Porth—"

"Hello, Andy."

She smiled at him. He was just as she'd pictured him, handsome in a fine-featured way with slightly pointed ears and a charming quirk to his mouth.

Aha. He's a fairy . . . whatever Branok and Gillan are . . .

"Ms Hart. Did you find the key?"

"I did. I'm inside now, as you can probably see." She raised the phone and turned it to let him see the interior of The Belfry. "I'm going to stay the night . . . probably two nights."

She tilted the screen back towards her face and saw him smiling back. He wore a short silver earring in a complicated design.

"Don't stay more than three nights unless you're willing to take up residence," he said.

"Why?"

"The place might get ideas about claiming you."

"Okay. Listen, Andy—before I make any kind of plans, I

need to know about zoning. Because I have difficulty working in full-time jobs, I started a small baking business to tide me over when I can't—er—function outside."

"The Halloween manifestation," he said, glancing off-camera as it were. "I'd love to know more about that."

"So would I—specifically how to end it. The Caledonian Curse is what I call it."

"Aye," he said, deadpan.

"Is there anything to prevent me from carrying on the business here? I'd want to expand, since part-time work might not be easy to get locally, and the Curse won't let me work full-time."

"I don't know the answer to that one offhand, but I'll check." He must have half-covered the microphone because she heard his voice, suddenly muffled, calling, "*Dellion, darling, can you check zoning laws for Fiddle Bay area?*" as he looked off-camera again.

Queenie, who had taken a strong liking to her contact during their brief telephonic acquaintance, gave him a dark mark. Addressing a PA or whatever she was as *darling* was—Lord! She bit her tongue to remind herself not to say something cutting. She hoped she could keep her face neutral.

After an interminable minute or so of murmured conversation, he came back onto the phone. "We're in luck, Ms Hart. My wife reminded me of someone in a house that used to be in our gift. She ran a successful art studio in Fiddle Bay for a couple of years. Since Kirk Circle is outside the town boundary, you're even more in the clear than she was."

"Thank you." Queenie felt simultaneously cheered and dashed. Andy Tredennick *was* as nice as he seemed. It was perfectly okay to *darling* a wife.

He was taken.

A dark-haired young woman loomed in behind him, grinning at Queenie and raising two thumbs in congratulation . . .

or possibly it was in the pleasure of ownership. Silver flashed on her wrists and around her wedding finger.

"All systems go, eh?" she said.

I'm sure it is, with you two . . .

Andy Tredennick had turned his face up with an adoring smile. His wife, having got her word in and possibly made her point, backed out of pick-up.

Queenie gave herself a mental shake. *First James Stuart and now Andy Tredennick . . . what are you like? What* is *it with these sudden connections you think you feel with strange men?*

She knew what it was. Since the Caledonian Curse had destroyed her relationship with her only two long-term boyfriends, she'd found it easier to stay single. James had invited her for a drink, even though she'd let fly with some Scottish invective. Andy's friendly interest in the Curse had shown her a possible future she'd almost given up on.

You are so pathetic, Queenie Hart.

But then, maybe it was time to stop being pathetic.

Instead of keeping under wraps, talk about it. Flaunt it. Better yet, go out with someone who understands these things already. Someone like Andy – but not already committed.

She realised he was looking perplexed. Presumably she was sitting with her mouth half-open and the stunned-mullet look of realisation on her face.

She said a belated goodbye and ended the call.

Chapter Eleven: Decision

Queenie Hart. August, 2021

Queenie spent the whole three days at The Belfry, eating the supplied food and exploring her environs.

No one knocked on her door. No one unlocked it with a master key and barged in, hoping to catch her baking at a volume that couldn't be pleaded as personal use. It was quiet, but just half an hour's walk from town.

The site of the old rectory showed no signs of imminent development, and the graveyard, which embraced both blocks in its curving outer wall, proved satisfactorily historical. The most recent burial she found was fifty years old, suggesting there wouldn't be too many bereft mourners visiting, and absolutely no hearses gliding around the circle.

The dodgy phone reception turned out to be centred on one small area under the trees, so she was confident about staying in touch with the outer world.

The relative proximity of Oakengrove could be useful, since either the managers or some of their guests might potentially become customers for her luxury tarts. The main festival, the *Oakengrove Experience* as the bus driver had classed it, was in late September this year. That was too close for comfort, but it should be safely outside the range of the Caledonian Curse.

On her second full day, she walked into Fiddle Bay and made a quiet reconnaissance. There was a bakery in the main street, but it was called *Our Daily Bread* and it featured artisan breads, pies and small cakes. Not a tart or a flan in sight.

Queen of Tarts would complement it nicely, and she'd not be treading on local toes.

She looked about in vain for the art studio Andy mentioned. Eventually, she asked a middle-aged woman who was wheeling a bicycle.

"Excuse me."

The woman made a *who, me?* face, then smiled. "Yes?"

"Someone told me there was an art studio somewhere around here."

"If you mean Elf-Made Art, it was here until a few months ago."

"I see. Why did it close?"

"It didn't. Quite the reverse. The owner got married, and she and her husband shifted the studio down the coast. They still own the building I think . . . some of the family lives there." She smiled again. "If you look up the website, I'm sure it'll have contact details. Elf-Made Art." She spelled it.

"Thank you," Queenie said.

"I hope you didn't come here especially," the woman said.

"Oh—no. I'm hoping to move here, and someone said there was a studio, that's all."

"I don't think that one's available," the woman said.

Queenie perceived she'd got hold of the wrong end of the stick. "Thanks anyway." She handed the woman one of her courtesy cards. "Maybe I'll see you sometime."

She wandered down to the cove. The beach was shingle, and the waves made the pebbles rattle. The scent of brine blew in her face. She'd always loved Sydney for its harbour, but here was the open sea. A young couple appeared as if from nowhere, walking hand in hand away from a dark tumble of rock. The girl twinkled with silver chains.

Queenie loitered to watch as they passed her by. The boy, brown-haired and lanky, glanced at her, down at his girl, and then back again.

His pause caught the girl's attention and she, too, looked at Queenie. Her face went haughty with pretended outrage and then she laughed and gave her boyfriend a great dig in the ribs. She held her free hand out in front of him, forming a circle with her thumb and second finger.

He cowered, laughing, and grabbed the hand to kiss.

What was that about?

Queenie saw the girl toss her head, making a short earring twinkle as her dark hair swung aside.

She's whatever Andy and his wife are. Whatever Branok are Gillan are . . . He's . . . not.

She half smiled, remembering the adage that if you heard a new word, you'd soon hear it again.

Fairies are among us.

Well, she'd known that already, but she'd never understood how literal it was, or what to look out for.

She walked back up to the post office, to look up the timetable for the bus she would take the next day . . . or the one after.

As if she'd called it into being, the minibus buzzed up, swinging into the space where she was about to read the plastic-covered timetable.

Queenie waited for three people to descend and one to get in and then she hopped up onto the bottom step.

"Excuse me."

"Hm?" The driver was poking at an electronic device on his dashboard.

"What time does the last bus to Borrowdale Junction leave?"

"This is it," he said, still poking. He glanced at her and then away. "Or it will be, after I've done the Oakengrove leg and am coming back the other way. Have you got a ticket?"

"No, I want to catch it tomorrow, or the next day."

"In that case, check the weekend timetable. It's on the

post."

"I was about to, when you got in the way," Queenie said.

The bus driver hit a lever and the door began to slide closed.

Queenie stepped back and down in a hurry.

"Well!"

She was reminded of the way she'd closed the door on Angel Petty. It was less pleasant to be on the receiving end.

Maybe the driver had done it by accident. He'd been kind to his less-able passengers, so she gave him the benefit of the doubt. That was, if he was the same driver. She couldn't tell. She realised she had zero memory of what the driver from the junction had looked like . . . not old, since he'd hopped in and out of the bus with alacrity, but—oh, he'd worn an outsized cap. This one did too, but maybe there was more than one and they all wore caps?

She walked back out along October Road to The Belfry, carrying fresh supplies.

It was a pleasant walk, but by the time she reached Kirk Circle her shoulder ached from the uneven weight of her bag.

Maybe if she hadn't snapped at the bus driver, he might have given her another lift.

Or maybe the one he'd already given her on Thursday had made him late for his pick-up at Oakengrove . . . if he was the same man.

If I do this . . . if I move here to The Belfry, I'll need transport.

A bike might work, she thought, remembering the woman she'd given the card to. Or a scooter. On the other hand, being able to deliver her wares would get her more orders and she couldn't do that on a bike. Scooter and trailer?

A small van would do. She had a licence, but having lived in the CBD since leaving home, she'd rarely needed to use it.

The bus driver had said there was no car hire, but she thought she'd be able to pick up a vehicle with the savings of the first three months' rent.

Registration, insurance . . . servicing. Petrol. Oh, dear.

She sighed. Every advantage had its associated downfall.

But wait . . . I'll save on public transport.

Maybe it would all balance out, and even come down on her side.

She slept comfortably at The Belfry, listening to the sigh of wind in the dark trees.

The caw of the crows or ravens began to feel friendly. Magpies trilled in the dawn.

After the third night, the idea of returning to Mother Goose Lane held no appeal.

She called Porthwellian Tredennick before remembering it was Sunday, and obviously no one would be there.

"Porthwellian Tredennick, Androw Tredennick speaking . . ."

"Really? You work Sundays?"

He chuckled. "Often the folk we deal with don't understand the concept of nine to five. What can I do for you, Ms Hart?"

"Queenie, please." She took a deep breath. "I've spent my three days here, and I'd like—I've decided—to take the three months. I hope that's still okay."

"Of course. We'll get the paperwork to you . . . but you'll have to wait for Oliver."

"Why?"

"Because he's the only one of us who has been there. The rest of us can't get a fix."

"You do realise you're talking gobbledegook."

"So Dellion says sometimes. That's my wife. Endellion. She who gave you some cheek the other day."

"She seems lovely."

He said, "No, she doesn't, and sometimes, she's not. But I love her anyway."

"I'm glad."

After a slightly awkward pause, he said, "I thought I was

being plain enough, though."

"Not even slightly," Queenie said. She bit her cheek to keep from grinning. She *did* like Andy Tredennick.

I wonder if he has a single brother . . .

She asked him.

"Well, yes, but he's nine years old."

"Big gap."

"Four sisters in between. And Dellion and I have two little lads."

It was on the tip of Queenie's tongue to say *you fairies are taking over the world,* but she caught herself in time.

"What did you mean about your senior partner having been here?" she asked, returning to safer ground.

"You really don't know? Okay—have you heard of conjuring?"

"Card tricks and interlocking rings?"

"No, the conjuring we do. Fay. You *did* know we're fay?"

"I'd noticed that, but conjuring . . . I don't think so." She grimaced. "The only fay I actually know are Branok St Ives and his wife, and I've met them only a handful of times."

"You undoubtedly know a lot more that those," Andy said.

"Maybe, but they must be still in the closet."

"It's not—never mind. To get back to the point of conjuring, I'm not even going to try to tell you over the phone. I'll text you something that will explain it far better than I, or Dellion, or even Oliver could. Go home and sort yourself out. Be back at The Belfry for your three months as soon as you can."

"It's really going to happen for me?"

"It really is."

"Thanks, Andy. There's just one thing—"

"What's that?"

"What *are* you?"

"A very junior partner in Porthwellian Tredennick."

"That's what you do. What *are* you?"

"Oh, I see. You're enquiring after my order. I'm a pisky

man—a fullblood. *Nos da."*

The call cut off.

Queenie felt little the wiser, but she opened the message when it came.

To her surprise, it contained a single line.

Got lost in links. All will be revealed when your belfry-warming gift arrives. Andy and Dellion.

Chapter Twelve: The Fixer

Queenie Hart. August, 2021

Any wobbles Queenie might have had when she was back in Sydney were crushed when she encountered her landlady's latest communication—an envelope shoved under the door.

She picked it up and read, without much surprise, that she'd been issued a notice to quit, effective immediately.

A few words, savagely underlined, stood out. *Broken the terms of the lease. Refused a reasonable request to cease and desist. Caused a nuisance. Actions encouraging vermin – to whit, a plague of ants.*

Queenie's initial indignation faded. The ants had arrived in a jar of home-made jam someone had given her as a sample. Finding it spoiled, she'd binned the whole jar, and bin escapees had turned up in her kitchen for weeks afterwards.

Technically, she *had* broken, or at least bent, the terms of the lease.

I don't sell from the unit–I take it to the market.

That was probably splitting hairs.

Never mind . . .

She was highly tempted to hire a Moving Marty van and flit by night, but she supposed she'd better be civil. After all, she wanted her bond back.

Angel Petty told her she could whistle for her bond.

Queenie pointed out that it was supposed to cover damage to structures and furnishings, of which there was none apart from *normal wear and tear.*

Ms Petty accused her of obstruction and threatening behaviour . . . and so Queenie gave in. She despised herself for doing so, but she conceded the bond, wished her landlady more joy of her next tenant, and promised to be gone forever within twenty-four hours.

The expression on the woman's face almost made it worth the hassle.

It was unfortunate that Queenie was tall and statuesque with big hips and a generous bosom. Angel Petty was pint-sized, slight, and barely cast a shadow. If anyone saw them having a verbal altercation, they'd inevitably conclude that Queenie was the aggressor.

A call to Moving Marty brought the unwelcome news that the first available vehicle could be collected next Wednesday . . . no, *not* the day after tomorrow . . . that was *this* Wednesday.

"But I need it today . . . tomorrow morning at the latest," she pleaded.

"No can do," the receptionist responded. "All our vehicles are out. We're always booked out days, if not weeks, ahead."

Then you should have more vehicles . . .

Queenie said, "Do you know any other companies who might have something available?"

"It's not our policy to recommend our competition."

"I suppose not." *And I will not be recommending you.* She hung up and scrolled through ads for vehicle hire.

An hour later, she'd got nowhere. She suspected removalist companies didn't want to take on such a small job.

"*Dammit* – why does everyone have to be so obstructive?" She was about to give up when she spotted a small ad. *In Sydney area and in a Fix? Need help today? Call the Fixer on 0417FIXER.*

What did she have to lose?

She called the number.

"Fixer."

"I'm in a fix. I have to be out of my unit in downtown Sydney within twenty-three hours."

"You need a place to live?"

"I have a place, up near Fiddle Bay. I need someone with a small truck or a van to get my stuff there. I don't have a car and I can't handle it all on public transport."

"Okay."

"Okay what?" she asked, confused.

"I can fix that. Text me the address and I'll be with you within . . . say . . . a couple of hours."

"Thanks. That's great."

She didn't ask the cost, because she knew it would be enormous, but after the stand-off with Angel Petty, she couldn't wait to leave.

She ended the call and texted the address. She got a brief *Okay* back and then began sorting what she needed to take.

Clothing. Her old chest. Baking gear. Non-perishable food. Books. A mother-of-millions plant her mum had left with her. Shoes. Paperwork. Great-Grandmother Elizabeth's clock.

She piled everything in the middle of the floor, and then she began a mostly unsuccessful scout-around for empty boxes. A single clothes basket and her suitcase were less than adequate.

Should have asked the Fixer to bring me some boxes.

Pillowcases!

That reminded her of bedding and linen, so she parcelled some of the loose items in that.

The Fixer tapped on the door before she was ready, but she admitted to herself that she could never be *ready* until she had boxes or crates.

She began trying to explain before he was even through the door.

He heard her out until she faltered to a stop.

"This is a dog's breakfast," he said, looking about.

"I know."

"I have boxes. You pack. I'll stack."

Queenie watched him gather an untidy bundle of bedding. He went out, and a few moments later, she turned to see five sturdy cardboard flat packs on the floor behind her.

She configured one of them and thrust in books, cutlery, baking trays, cans, and jars of jam as fast as she could. If she was paying by the hour, she wanted to get out as quickly as possible.

As she filled each box, she turned to the next, leaving it to the Fixer to get it out to his truck.

He must be stronger than he looks.

When he spoke to her again, she almost jumped out of her skin. "The washing machine? The dryer?"

"They're not mine."

"Have you left anything in them?"

"No."

"Fridge?" He opened the door. "Ooh, tarts!"

Hurriedly, Queenie removed milk, wilted salad, eggs and some sad carrots from the shelves. She dropped things in the green waste bin and used up the milk in two final cups of coffee.

"Tarts," he said again, accepting a chipped mug she wasn't taking with her. "May I take my free sample?"

Queenie wasn't aware that she'd offered him one, but he might have picked up one of her cards somewhere or spotted the magnets on the fridge. "Help yourself. I'll only tip them otherwise. They're a few days old."

He bent past her and removed the snap-lid box of pastries from the almost-empty fridge. He crammed one into his mouth and then opened the freezing compartment and dealt with the contents. "This your own fridge?"

"No. White goods came with the unit."

"Okay, unplug it and give it a wipe down. Lemon juice, bicarb, or vanilla essence . . . Leave the door open. Take your magnets off."

So he did spot them.

He snapped a couple free. "Queen of Tarts."

"Yes," she said.

"Brilliant. Bet you get some interesting comments on that trading name. Anything under the sink?"

"Gloves, bucket, mop—you've done this before."

"More often than you can count. It's surprising what people forget. Clothes pegs, love letters, curtains—the dog. The eleven-year-old who was sent to play with the neighbours."

"The curtains aren't mine. I don't have a dog, or an eleven-year-old."

He absently put another tart in his mouth.

"Any hidden treasures?" he mumbled around it. "Jewellery stashed in a concealed safe, pictures on the wall, favourite shoes under the bed, biscuit tins of cash buried beneath the doorstep, earring dropped down the back of the couch, silver teapots up the chimney . . ."

Queenie gasped and hurried to unhook the landscape Great-Granny Adelaide Southey had owned from the bedroom door. She already had Great-Granny Elizabeth Mack's clock, and the vase and bracelet belonging to Great-Grannies Mary Hart and Victoria Grant.

Her inheritance, she supposed. She wondered how hungry she'd have to be to sell the clock, which was the only one likely to be worth any more than retro-treasure prices.

Maybe she ought to have locked her nest egg away in an untouchable account rather than pushing Ms Petty into giving her notice.

"Vacuum cleaner yours?"

"Yes."

"Plug it in, and I'll run it over the floor. You do a last whip round and toss anything you want to keep in that spare box."

Queenie did so, and then, satisfied she had everything she needed and had left the remainder in good order, she stepped out of her unit for the last time.

The Fixer followed her, carrying the vacuum clearer and chewing the last of the tarts.

Pity. She might have left that last one, crumbling at the edges, in the middle of the table to attract ants as some sort of gesture.

Queenie turned to look at the moving truck and stalled in place.

It wasn't a truck or a van, but a small green bus.

"Don't forget to hand the key in," the Fixer said.

"Oh. No." She walked the short distance to the unit where Angel Petty lurked, scenting the air for illicit baking activities, and she knocked on the door.

There was no answer.

She knocked again.

The Fixer came up behind her. "Do you need to hand that over in person? Pick up a bond or anything? Sign a quit form?"

She shook her head.

"No letterbox?"

"No."

Probably afraid someone will shove something unmentionable through it.

"Push it under the door. Label it first." He handed her a small, punched luggage label and a fountain pen, carved from something that looked like high-end bamboo.

Souvenir of a tropical holiday?

Mechanically, Queenie wrote down the unit number and Ms Petty's name. Underneath, she wrote *Returned key* and added her name, the date, and time. She fastened the key to the label and bent to push it under the door.

"Wait. Give me your phone."

She handed it over. The Fixer stood back. "I'm going to film you putting it under the door so there's absolutely no doubt you did it. Give it a good shove so it disappears. There."

He straightened, stared down at the phone for a second and then he handed it back. "Let's go. Do you need a hand? A tissue? A wise aphorism about doors that open and close? A hug?"

She shook her head.

"Okay. Let's get you back to The Belfry before dark."

Queenie got into the bus. She didn't ask how he knew she wanted to go to The Belfry. After all, he'd driven her there four days before, and conducted her from the Fiddle Bay post office to meet the Sydney train at Borrowdale Junction that morning.

The strange thing was that she hadn't recognised him until she saw the green bus.

To be fair, she'd been sitting behind him when they left the junction and had been focused on her malfunctioning three-six-five when she embarked, and on her luggage and the steep steps when she disembarked.

But still . . . she must have seen his face when she gave him the fare and thanked him for the ride.

She pictured other people she'd encountered equally briefly. Branok, Gillan . . . their dog, Lady Velvet . . . James Stuart, Andy and Dellion Tredennick . . . even the young couple on the beach and the woman with the bike in Fiddle Bay. All their faces came readily to mind.

She looked sideways to refresh her memory of the Fixer's appearance, but there was nothing to hook to a memory—aside from the large cap. It probably wasn't the same cap he'd worn before, because this one was printed with *The Fixer,* and she thought she might have noticed that.

The Fixer drove out through the familiar suburb to the highway. He obeyed the rules of the road, showing no impatience at slow-to-change lights or those that flashed red on his approach. The silence began to get uncomfortable.

Finally, Queenie said, "Mitch?"

"Yeah?"

"Why—I mean, you *are* the bus driver from Fiddle Bay, right?"

"Sure," he said. She thought that was all she was going to get, but he glanced at her sideways under the beak of his preposterous cap. "Driving a dozen or so passengers—and that's on a *good* day—doesn't constitute a living wage. It hardly puts petrol in Ethel." He patted the steering wheel. "I like to eat."

"I suppose so," she said.

He certainly liked to eat my tarts.

"I mean—I *really* like to eat. I collect free samples every chance I get."

"Fair enough." So did she.

"Sometimes people even offer them to me, the way you did."

The bus continued up the coast and then, to Queenie's surprise, the Fixer turned off at Borrowdale Junction.

"We're going the wrong way."

"Got to pick up some passengers," he said briefly.

She could scarcely object, considering she'd benefited from his willingness to deviate from the timetable on her first trip.

The train came in seven minutes later, and three people boarded the bus, glancing incuriously at Queenie.

"Mitch."

"Hi, Kez. Post Office stop okay, or do you want me to swing round to your street?"

"Would you, love?"

"Just stay on and I'll drop you before I go to the big house."

"Ta. You're a lifesaver. When do you go off for your break?"

"October."

"Your cousin taking over again?"

"Same deal as usual."

The elderly woman subsided behind Queenie with a sigh.

"Anyone for the big house?" the Fixer asked.

No one said anything.

"Okay."

Having dropped various passengers in Fiddle Bay, they drove on.

Queenie ventured, "Will you have time to drop me at The Belfry before you pick up people from the big house?"

"Yes."

"What about my stuff . . . it'll take a while to unload."

"That's okay."

She subsided.

It'd better not rain while all those boxes are outside.

This time, they drove right around the circle to The Belfry, and the Fixer parked the bus at the gate. "Got the key?"

She glanced at the building. "It's around the side."

"You get it and I'll unload."

Queenie walked around to the side, where she found the key still, or maybe again, clipped to the old clothesline.

She removed it and returned to unlock the main door, blinking with confusion as she saw her belongings already arranged on either side of the shallow steps.

How the hell did he do that? Is he an octopus?

She turned amazed eyes to the Fixer, who had bent to lift the first flat pack.

"If you unlock, I can get these things inside for you, but I'll have to leave you to unpack," he said.

"Oh—thanks."

She undid the door and turned on the power.

"Where do you want 'em?"

She indicated the foyer. "Here's fine."

"You won't be able to get past them."

"Main room, then, if you have time."

He carried the first box in and set it inside.

Queenie picked up the clothes basket and then a couple of lighter items.

"Check the bus. Make sure there's nothing left under the

seat or on the parcel rack," he said.

About to object, she remembered Great-Grandmother Adelaide's painting, which had almost been left behind in the bedroom back at the unit.

A quick inspection assured her that her first impulse had been correct. She had everything.

She returned to find all the large boxes in the main room. Her heavy wooden chest was in the mezzanine bedroom, positioned against the wall.

He must move like oiled lightning!

The Fixer was back by his bus, messing with his phone. He looked up as Queenie came alongside, frowning slightly as if wondering what she wanted.

"I'd offer you another cup of coffee, but I know you have to go," she said.

"Nine minutes," he said.

"What—"

"To be at the big house. That's not enough time to boil a jug from cold, and there won't be any hot water yet. Raincheck?"

"Okay," she said.

He swiped the phone and dropped it into his pocket.

"Do I pay now, or will you send me an account?" she asked.

"Whichever."

He looked up at her from under the cap.

What's with him? On the spectrum? Shy?

She said, as patiently as she could, "I can pay now if you tell me the amount."

"Didn't I?"

"Not yet."

He took out his phone and poked it again. Then he pulled out an old-fashioned carbon receipt book and his wooden pen and poised it expectantly.

Queenie waited in gathering exasperation. "Mitch. *Tell me*

the amount."

He jumped. Out came the phone.

"No, don't start again with the phone. Just give me a figure, and then say *cash* or *card.*"

"Either." He gave her a figure.

It was high enough, but not as high as she'd expected, considering he'd been so efficient and so patient and had done the job *today*. No *next Wednesday week* or *dump-and-run* or *I'm not licenced to lift that*, or *sign this indemnity.*

She opened her purse and took out some notes.

He accepted them, hesitated, and handed one back.

"What's that for?"

"Tarts."

"I told you, I'd have had to bin them if you hadn't eaten them."

He shook his head. "That was my free sample. This is for more tarts."

"I don't have any—"

"When you make them."

"How many do you want? Which style?"

He gave her a now-you-see-it, now-you-don't grin.

"However many this will buy me. And surprise me."

"How—"

"You've got my number." He sprang into the driver's seat, closed the door and drove away.

Queenie stared after him, open-mouthed.

Chapter Thirteen: Signing the Lease

Queenie Hart. August, 2021

The remainder of August passed quickly and pleasantly. Queenie, released from the tyranny of Angel Petty, but aware of the need to get to work, spent a few days getting straight. Unpacking took much longer than packing had, because she had to choose a place for each item and arrange it properly to avoid double or triple handling.

A packet of papers turned up on the main room table one afternoon at the end of the month when she came back from a walk to town. She read through them carefully. They were a lease agreement for her first three months, but there wasn't much to be learned aside from what Andy Tredennick had sent her via text message.

She called Andy to ask who had delivered them, saying she'd have been there if she'd known when to expect them.

And intercepted whoever it was at the door . . . I've had enough of landlords who just walked in with Ms Petty.

Andy sighed. "Oliver, of course. I told you before."

"Am I being exasperating?" she asked.

Andy said, "Even if you were, you have a right to be. Queenie, you absolutely have the right to ask for what you want. Wish for it, even."

She laughed. "Oddly enough, I was once offered a wish by a living statue."

"Did you use it?"

"Yes, in the manner of speaking, though I'm not sure if it

did him any good."

There was a brief scuffle and a sudden clonk. The call fell out.

Before Queenie had time to feel insulted, her phone buzzed, requesting a video call. She accepted.

Andy's head swam into the pick-up, half-obscured by another face, beaming at her.

Queenie took the initiative . . . or was it the offensive? "Hello, Dellion."

The woman made her triumphant thumbs up gesture. "Hi, Queenie. How's the new place?"

"Brilliant."

"Mwah!" Dellion blew her a kiss, leaned back, and twined an arm around Andy's neck.

Okay . . . so she's going to be friendly, but she's also – what? Reminding me he's taken?

Queenie sidestepped the subtext.

Cheyenne apart, for some odd reason, wives and girlfriends often supposed she was about to flirt with their men.

Oh, who was she kidding?

It was the downside of being blonde, curvaceous, and tall.

Andy spat out some of Dellion's hair. "We need to talk about your housewarming present."

Queenie was about to question that, but Dellion said, "Just so you know, I'm not a stalky-minx who can't stay away from her man's place of work. I'm a partner in this firm, and technically senior to my man. Oliver is my great-grandfather. My brother—"

"Dellion, she doesn't need to know all that."

Queenie broke in quickly. All this affectionate togetherness was tweaking her loneliness. "How do I stand with putting hooks or nails in the wall to hang things?" she asked at random.

"The rule of thumb is to treat the place as if it were your own—*except* we'd prefer you refrain from making major structural changes."

"Um?"

"He's being pompous. He means, don't knock any walls down or rip up the floorboards," Dellion said.

"I wouldn't dream of it."

"Major cosmetic changes, such as painting the interior pearl pink—" Andy began.

"—are verboten," Queenie suggested.

"I was going to say, *are to be left until or unless you renew your lease.*"

"For another three months?" She already knew she wanted to stay. Andy and Dellion, and even the invisible Oliver, were much nicer landlords than Angel Petty. The Tredennick double act might wear thin if she had to encounter it often, but it was entertaining in the short term.

"Three—six—twelve months . . . or you could go for a circumstantial lease."

"What's that?"

"It means you can arrange to stay until or unless your circumstances change . . . for example, if you get a long-term job overseas—"

"Or if you marry someone from somewhere else and decide to live there with him . . . or her," Dellion said.

"I'd like that!"

"What . . . to marry a him or a her and go—"

"*No,* to have a circumstantial lease!"

"Ask us after your three months," Andy said.

A yell and a bang out of pick-up brought Dellion to sudden alert. "Gotta go. The boys are doing something horrible with Great-Grandad Bod's sextant. Mwah!" She threw another kiss, slid off her husband's lap, and vanished.

Queenie said, "What do I do with these papers? Or do you have to go and untangle your kids and your great-grandad's sextant?"

"Dellion can manage. He was *her* ancestor, not mine. Sign them—the papers, not the boys—and get them witnessed, and then you can post them to us, or else leave them on the table where you found them. Text when you do it, and Oliver will snag them from there."

That sounded as if Oliver Porthwellian would walk in and pick them up, but the man was ninety-six and he didn't believe in mobile phones. Still, he had evidently delivered them, so who knew?

"I don't understand."

"When your housewarming present arrives you will . . . if you read it. You won't learn by osmosis."

"I suppose Oliver will deliver that, too," she said.

"No . . . that's what I need to talk about. It'll be put in the post soon. Do you want to change the postal address you put on record?"

"Glory yes! I don't think Branok and Gillan want my housewarming gift landing in their letter-box."

"Okay—done. Your official address is now The Belfry."

Another yell and a call of *Andeeeee!* made him wince. "*Nos da*." He hung up.

Queenie frowned. What was that last bit? She shrugged. The folk at Porthwellian Tredennick were more than a wee bit odd.

So was the Fixer.

She thought about his face and couldn't recall it at all.

He can't be handsome or ugly, or very old, or very young. I'd remember. He must be—just ordinary. Blokey, like Dad, but not too much like Dad, or I'd have noticed. Next time, I'll make sure I look at him properly.

She dug a pen out of the Cloisonne vase that used to belong to Great-Grandmother Mary Hart and pulled the lease agreement into position. She read it through again and was about to sign it when she remembered it had to be witnessed.

She tapped the pen against her chin and then she

remembered that the small independent supermarket had agreed to deliver her order. She could easily carry supplies for herself in a backpack, but when it came to baking, she needed to buy in bulk. For an extra ten dollars paid when she did her shopping, the check-out man, Duncan Dee, who was also the owner-manager of *Fiddle-de-Dee Groceries,* had promised same-day delivery.

Excellent. I'll grab him when he gets here.

Queenie had bagged a stall at the Saturday market being held that week on the minute village green, but she hadn't yet cracked the chicken-and-egg problem of getting her tarts to market without paying more for transport than she could earn in profit. Living rent-free at The Belfry was lovely, but she couldn't hope for walk-in traffic while situated at the end of a road leading nowhere else. There was no way she could afford a shopfront in Fiddle Bay, even if one fell vacant.

The arrangement she'd had with Finger-Puppet Lin in Sydney had worked well enough, but she had no circle of acquaintance in Fiddle Bay yet.

Let's face it – no one is going to want to drive two-and-a-half-kay every time I have a delivery to make.

She might have to call the Fixer again. He'd got her out of one major fix.

She hadn't saved his text, but maybe the number was somewhere in the bowels of her phone. If all else failed, she could picket the post office bus stop until the green bus—Ethel—rolled up.

She had just removed a test batch of tarts from the oven when someone tapped on the door.

Queenie picked up the lease agreement and headed for the door in a hurry in case the prepaid delivery driver dropped the stores and scarpered before she could intercept him . . . or her. It could easily be a her.

"Just a minute," she said pleasantly, catching him—it was a him—in the act of turning aside from the door. "Would you—"

He swivelled to face her, shoving back a cap emblazoned with the name and logo of the Fiddle Bay supermarket.

It wasn't Duncan Dee, who was moon-faced and stocky.

Queenie glanced beyond him to his vehicle, a small green bus.

"Mitch Fixer?"

Really?

"Do I smell tarts?" he asked. It had to be a rhetorical question, because the rich scent of shortcrust pastry and fruit permeated The Belfry and oozed enticingly from the open door.

"You do, but they're still at the fragile stage where they break if you look at them funny—"

He smiled.

"May I come in and test that pronouncement for veracity?"

About to disallow him, Queenie remembered she owed him some tarts and needed a favour. Besides, he'd already been inside . . . and after his methodical stripping down of her unit in Mother Goose Lane, he knew her domestic secrets anyhow.

She stepped back.

The oven pinged on a second batch of tarts.

"I have to—"

"Go ahead. I'll get your order in."

Six large boxes of supplies should take him a while to shift, but when she turned from peeping through the oven window, he had the boxes lined up on her bench.

She frowned.

Before she could ask—or even formulate a viable question—he'd moved to hover over the tray of tarts cooling on the rack.

"Are these for me?"

"Sure, if you like. They're a mixed test batch to see how the oven performs."

He picked one up and opened his mouth.

"Wait! That jam's still hot!"

He glanced at her. "I know. I was just inhaling the scent."

"Most people do that with their nose."

"The tastebuds on the roof of the mouth work well for hot jam."

"If you have time for a cup of tea or coffee, they'll be cool enough to pack," she said. She switched the jug on. "Mitch?"

"Yeah?"

"Why are you delivering my groceries?"

"It's my job."

"But you're the bus driver. And the Fixer. And now you're delivering flour and eggs for the supermarket. Just what is your official job title?"

He gave her a vague smile. "It changes, depending on which hat I'm wearing."

"Literally or figuratively?"

He removed his supermarket cap. "Both, I suppose."

"How many hats do you have?"

He shrugged. "A few. They help me keep things straight." He seemed to consider for a few seconds. Then he added, "I have a hat wall at home with the days of the week. I use it to make a hat graph and pin my shifts to the hats I need each day."

"Most people keep timetables in their phones," Queenie said.

"I do that, too, but sometimes I lose them. One September I put my phone down and didn't track it down until November."

Queenie spooned coffee into mugs, wondering if she believed him and whether it mattered. "While you're here, would you witness my signature on the lease for this place?"

"Is that what you were clutching when you came to the door?"

"Yes."

"I will, if you're sure you want to do that," he said.

"I want to do it. Even if I didn't, I'm committed now." She found the pen and signed her name and the date. "Here, where it says *signed in the presence of,*" she said. "Sign and then print your name." She pushed the lease towards him.

He took it, turned to the front page and began to read.

"You don't need to *read* it." She didn't want him knowing her business. He was bound to think it weird that she wasn't paying any rent for three months, and when he got to the *payment in kind* or *peppercorn* clause in the case of a renewal, he'd think her shady—or soft in the head.

He looked up. "I don't sign things unless I've read them. If you don't want me to read this, then I can't sign."

"You're not signing the lease. You're simply signing a declaration that you witnessed me writing my signature."

"Oh. In that case . . ." He flipped to the back page and scribbled a signature, using his own pen. Then he printed his name. "Envelope?"

She handed it over, and he thrust the papers in and pressed the seal.

"Want me to put this in the post?"

"No thanks. I have to leave it on the table in the main room to be—er—collected."

"Okay. Better put it there now before it attracts jam."

That was a reasonable idea, so she did as he suggested.

When she returned, he had a tart in his mouth.

"Mitch?"

He rolled his eyes and jerked a thumb towards his bulging cheek. Then he chewed a few times and swallowed.

"Best—tart—ever."

"Really?" She was pleased.

"Much better than the ones from your fridge at the other place. Fresher. Warmer. Moister."

Queenie stared him down.

He looked away. "What else did you want? You seemed to be about to ask me something."

"How do you know?"

"You said *Mitch* and then did a little intake of breath."

"I have booked a stall at the market on the green on Saturday morning," she said.

"Tart stall?"

"Yes. That's why I needed the supplies today."

"Since it's your first stall here, you'll want signage, and some cards."

"I have those. I used to go round markets in the city."

"And order forms, so people who buy samples can order in bulk for parties and take orders from their friends for a tiny commission. You could also do regular orders at a discount."

She'd never thought of that, but she said, "I have those too. I print my own."

"You're all set, then."

"I've been doing this for a while, off and on, Petty permitting," she said patiently.

"So what's the problem? Obviously not the tarts . . . do you do healthy option tarts?"

"*Yes.* Gluten free and all sorts of other things free, though the texture suffers."

"It would. My granny—" He broke off.

She said, "I used to get a ride to markets in Sydney with a friend who made finger puppets." *Friend* was stretching it, she supposed, although Lin Finger-Puppet had been obliging.

Comprehension showed in his eyes. "So you need tart-transport."

"Yes." She hit one fist into the other palm. "It seems ridiculous. I'm less than three kay from the village green. That's *nothing* on a fine day, but I can't bundle dozens of tarts up in a backpack. They're fragile. I could carry one or two batches, but I need to have plenty of stock to justify the cost of the stall."

"You could hire me to drive you," he said.

"I know, but it's such a small job it'd hardly be worthwhile for you. I used to give Lin—my friend—petrol money and tarts, but—"

"Tarts." His voice took on a greedy note.

Queenie ignored that. "If things work out in the tart department, I might get a van, but not yet."

He nodded thoughtfully, snagging another tart. He inhaled. "That's not marmalade."

"No, citrus jelly. I call that the cathedral sunshine tart."

"I can see why." He bit in. His eyes rolled again.

Queenie watched him eat.

She loved watching people eat. Her boyfriends had found that cute at first, then off-putting. Her female friends found it plain creepy.

The Fixer picked up another tart. "What's this one called? Ruby Tuesday?"

She laughed. "That's a starter tart . . . the basic recipe. I made that to judge the oven and the—"

"Ambiance." He nodded. "Too good to be a starter tart though. I recommend a better name. Do you have mouth-watering descriptions on your order forms?"

"Of course." She hadn't yet, but she would have.

After he'd worked his way through six tarts and a second cup of coffee, he asked, "Do you have any objection to tricycles?"

"You mean those ultra-light aircraft?"

"No, I mean three-wheeled bikes—two wheels at the back and one at the front."

"Should I?"

He dusted flour off his fingers. "Some people do."

"I had one when I was three."

"I was talking about the adult size. They're sturdy enough

to take a closed-in trailer. Some people tow their children in them, or their shopping."

"Oh! You mean I could use one to transport my tarts."

"You can get them with baskets that take about twenty kilograms, but a properly sprung trailer is a better option."

Queenie pictured it. "I'm here for three months, with an option for more if I want, and this would give me a chance to test the waters."

"That's the idea." He added, musingly, "A coach and four would be better. You could arrive like royalty with a herald—*make way for the Queen of Tarts!*"

She said, "I don't suppose there are any local suppliers?"

"Oddly enough, I do know someone with a coach and four. Shall I—"

"I meant suppliers of tricycles."

She'd love to hire the coach and four, but she knew that would cost more than she'd make in a month—especially the month that loomed far too near in her future.

"If you don't insist on *new,* my cousin Georgiana has one she used when her children were small. She doesn't use it now, but if I know her, it's greased up and swathed in hessian in the barn."

"Do you think she'd sell it to me?"

He shrugged. "How would a long loan suit you? I should think she'd be pleased to have it used."

Queenie looked at him thoughtfully. "Why?"

"Huh?"

"Why are you being so helpful?"

"It's my nature." He smiled at her. "It isn't altruism. It's just a *thing*. I'm a fixer. I like to fix things. I also like tarts. An offer of tarts draws me the way the offer of fish draws a tomcat."

"I noticed. If you give me your cousin's details, I could get in touch."

"I can ask her myself. If she's happy with the idea, I can get it to you." He'd been leaning against the sink, but he propped himself back onto his feet. Maybe he'd noticed the none-too-subtle attempt to distance him. "I'd better go. Are those tarts cool enough to box up?"

"I expect so." Queenie hurriedly slotted together one of the cardboard boxes she used for one-off sales. "They'll freeze okay."

He took the box. "No need. I'll eat them—"

"Aren't you full?"

"Oh—yes. But I won't be later." He looked about. "I'll see you soon."

"Oh?"

"Bound to," he said. He put on his delivery cap and headed back to his bus with his box of tarts held in front of him in both hands.

Queenie watched him go. She twitched a smile as she remembered the pageboy at Julia's wedding who had carried the ring-cushion with just such careful concentration.

Then she texted Andy Tredennick to tell him the lease papers were tabled.

Then she considered Mitch the Fixer again.

He certainly loved her tarts. She'd never seen anyone else absorb them with so much enjoyment.

She still couldn't picture his face.

Chapter Fourteen: Bernie

Queenie Hart. September, 2021

The lease disappeared from the table in the main room a week later.

Queenie saw it happen, and it gave her a nasty shock.

It was a Wednesday, and she'd begun to wonder about getting to the market in a few days' time. She'd lucked out on the first market day, when the person who'd assigned her the stall called by to see if she needed any more information.

He was a white-haired man who reminded her a bit of her dad, and he'd brought his wife along because, he said, she was dying to see what The Belfry was like inside.

Queenie had a small, shamed thought that if she'd been less blonde, less tall and less shapely, perhaps the wife wouldn't have felt the need to come . . .

She mentally slapped her hand.

Bernard "Call me Bernie" Tucker said he and his wife both remembered The Belfry as a working church when they were children, but since it was outside the town boundary it didn't fall under the council jurisdiction, so he'd never had a chance to see the conversion.

Queenie gave them afternoon tea and buttered her bread assiduously by plying them with tarts—peppermint Irish shamrocks and Welsh dragons, which contained chili.

Call-me-Bernie, as the official information bureau for newcomers, explained that Fiddle Bay was a relaxed community.

"Mostly," his wife put in, leaning forwards and fixing

Queenie with the eyes of a friendly seagull. "We're far enough from the city to be autonomous . . . I mean, we have the festival at the big house, but we try to keep the local interest up. Family stuff, so people don't feel the need to keep heading south like lemmings. There's a Christmas Parade, egg hunts for the kiddies at Easter, and a fancy-dress ball and pumpkin carving competition at Halloween."

"We have a choir and Mums' Runs, and the Dad Ballet is always popular," Bernie said, deftly inserting his piece into his wife's flow of talk.

"Bernie started that, bless him," the wife inserted back in.

"Charity do," Bernie added. He accepted another tart. "We take it seriously."

"Really?"

"Oh, yes." He got up from the table and, to Queenie's amusement, he executed a *plié*, a *relevé* and a *sauté* in smooth succession.

He sat down again. "If we hammed it up and acted silly it wouldn't be nearly as entertaining."

"They've never had formal training, but the boys all do their best, bless them. They do all the proper exercises, warm-ups and that." Missus Bernie, whose name Queenie was struggling to remember, beamed with apparent pride.

"We're not twisting your arm to join in everything, but we hope you'll enjoy some of our activities," Bernie said, becoming formal.

"And that brings us to the market," Missus Bernie cut in.

"We know it can be a bit daunting—"

Missus Bernie grabbed the conversational ball back. "As it's your first week, we wondered if you'd like a bit of help. Our daughter, Nona, works at the big house. She takes their display and program down to the market once a month. If you like, she's happy to call for you and take you along, help you set up and introduce you to the other stallholders."

"Not every week, though," Bernie warned.

"That would be great," Queenie jumped in. She added, "I'm hoping to get a small van eventually, and I'm borrowing something in the meantime—at least I hope so—but I'm not really settled yet."

"Okey-dokey." Bernie went colloquial. He drained his tea and got to his feet. "Come on, Maur . . . Queenie's got a lot on her plate, so we'll stop bending her ears and leave her to it. Nona will call by about six o'clock on Saturday morning."

He headed for the door, and Queenie rose hurriedly to see them out.

Missus Bernie—Maureen—lingered. "It's good to have new blood in the bay, love, and we do hope you'll enjoy living here. You're welcome to join in, and you can always give Bernie or me a bell if you need to know anything. The info pack he left so subtly on his chair will tell you what's on and when, but don't worry, we won't keep dropping in or bothering you all the time."

"That's—"

"No, really. Let me put it this way. When our Nona was born, Bernie's mum came to me in the hospital—we stayed in for a few days then, not in and out the way you are now. She said she'd brought up six kiddies, and before that she'd looked after three younger brothers. She said she wasn't longing to mind Nona all the time, but she was there to help if I ever needed her. I had only to ask. She was a good, sensible woman. Bernie's just like her, and he's a credit to his upbringing."

She didn't wait for an answer but hurried to catch up with her husband.

Queenie watched them go and then she shook her head, slowly. *What an extraordinary couple.* And yet, they weren't. They were exactly the way the welcome committee to a community ought to be . . .

They were quite unlike Andy and Dellion Tredennick and Branok and Gillan St Ives, but still . . .

Another double act.

Nona, a cheerful woman in her forties, showed up before six, and said she was happy to show Queenie the ropes at the market. She also reiterated what her parents had said.

"It's a fine line between being welcoming and being pushy. Mum and Dad do their best, but sometimes . . ."

"They were entertaining," Queenie said.

Nona's eyes crinkled in a grin. "They're a bit oh-tee-tee at times, but yes, they're good value. Dad's soul longs for beautiful things, and he's got the sense to find it where he lives, and if it's not there, he makes it."

"The Dad Ballet?"

Nona gave a sudden hoot of laughter. "Shit yes! Sorry."

"Don't be. I sometimes curse in Gaelic."

"That's different. But yeah, the Dad Ballet is *enormous* around here. Dad even rounded up an old Russian from somewhere—the Dads are performing at Oakengrove this year. There was some controversy over whether they'd be allowed to—it's mostly indie bands who write their own stuff—but there was nothing in the rules to say they couldn't."

"I like that. Nothing in the rules to say they couldn't so they do," Queenie said.

"They do their own choreography," Nona said.

"No women?"

"There's nothing in the rules to say women can't join—or guys with no kids, come to that—"

At that point, they reached the market, where the early birds were setting up, so Queenie heard no more on the subject.

There were a few hitches on that first day, as all markets have their own unwritten rules and flavours, but business was brisk, and Queenie's courtesy cards and order forms were soon depleted. She knew that only a few of these would convert into future sales, and that she was benefiting from the value of novelty and kindness to a newcomer, but still, things were looking up.

She half-expected a visit from the tart-loving Fixer, but he didn't come. At least, she didn't see anyone wearing a preposterous cap, and the green bus was not in evidence.

It occurred to her that she might not have recognised him even if he had come unless he chose to give her cues. He probably didn't wear his caps off duty, and the bus was doubtless a work vehicle.

Maybe I offended him when I turned down his offer to hire him to get me to the market and then tried to get his cousin's details so I could deal with her directly.

He'd said he'd talk to his cousin about the tricycle, but if he had, she'd heard nothing about it.

With Saturday negotiated, she'd had a quiet Sunday and then made some personalised birthday tarts for a new customer.

The customer came to collect them and stayed for coffee.

On Wednesday, with another market closing in on her, Queenie found a local magazine called *Stradevarious* on her doorstep. She read it over breakfast and was touched to see a free puff for her tarts tucked in among the other local advertisements. A list of advertising prices appeared inside the magazine which, as well as having the expected news and information, was quite a fat production, including pieces from locals on subjects ranging from the habits of the Pacific Gull to the history of a shipwreck and a biography of the first settler at the bay. The broad range of contributors suggested the editorial staff wanted to keep the circulation up with copies sent to distant friends and relatives.

She'd just folded the magazine and laid it aside when her focus fell on the envelope holding the lease agreement.

Something tweaked at her mind, and she finally teased out

what it was.

A pen was clipped tidily to the envelope, and it wasn't one of hers. This one was made of wood—possibly bamboo.

The Fixer had used that to witness her signature. He'd left it behind, but why? By mistake? Deliberately?

If it had been a wallet or keys or a designer jacket, Queenie would have felt obliged to call him and to let him know where it was.

If it had been a box of matches, or a pair of old shoes or a gardening shirt, she'd have left it handy to give him . . . sometime.

A polished wooden fountain pen fell uncomfortably between the parameters.

She stared at it, trying once again to remember the Fixer's face. She remembered his hand holding the pen, and the way he'd slid the papers into the envelope and pressed the seal, but she couldn't see his face.

That was the point when she realised she didn't even know his full name.

Mitch was presumably short for Mitchell, but was that his first or last name? Some people did get called by a version of their surname—witness all the people known as Smitty or Robbie or Bart when their surnames with Smith or Roberts or Bartholomew.

So . . . what was the Fixer's name?

It would be easy enough to find out. All she had to do was to pull the papers out and look. She mightn't be able to make out his signature, but he'd printed the name as well.

He'd sealed the envelope, but she could undo that. If it tore, well, she'd just have to get another one. She unclipped the pen and laid it aside and then reached out to retrieve the papers.

She had just put her fingers on the envelope, pressing down to draw it across the table to where she was sitting, when it vanished.

She didn't see it go. It was just there one instant, sliding easily over the polished wood, and the next, she felt a slight drag of resistance as her fingertips met the table with no envelope to intervene.

Queenie uttered a squeak of shock and snatched her fingers back.

She stared at the bare table, then looked wildly about.

Common sense insisted the envelope must have blown off the table and out of sight. She peeped underneath and then walked around the whole room, but it was gone. It was a bright yellow A4 envelope, so it couldn't be lying quietly in a corner.

Queenie strained her brain trying to figure out what had happened.

She felt spooked and foolish in equal measures. Feeling spooked was natural when something disappeared while she was touching it, yet feeling spooked was foolish when it was a sunny morning in early spring, in her new and welcoming home.

Settle down.

She did her best, but the feeling of unease refused to go away. The Belfry was home, and she was more relieved than she could say to be clear of Angel Petty, but one thing kept sneaking back into her mind. It was the one thing she'd wilfully ignored in her haste to move into her new domain.

Branok St Ives had suggested The Belfry, but he'd stressed that she should take it on a short lease first. Gillan had said a previous tenant, or tenants, hadn't wanted to stay. Andy and Dellion had seemed positively delirious with joy when she agreed to sign the lease. Even the Fixer had implied that she might want to think hard.

What's wrong with this place?

What's its history?

Queenie felt chilled. The Belfry had been a church, complete with a rectory and graveyard. The rectory was gone . . .

pulled down or possibly burned . . . and the site cleared. The graveyard was disused. The Belfry *must* have been deconsecrated to render it available for secular use, but *why*?

Maybe something horrible happened here.

Maybe it's haunted.

Branok had said there was no such thing as ghosts, but he didn't know everything. He hadn't known about her Caledonian Curse. Andy had said it was rare. She wondered if he and Dellion believed in ghosts.

I'll ask them.

But first, she decided to try a source closer to hand.

The *Stradevarious* still lay on the table. She put her hand out, almost expecting it to vanish under her touch. It remained reassuringly corporeal, and she opened it and turned to the advertising rates and editorial contact.

There was a phone number.

Queenie made the call.

"*Stradevarious.*"

She had the right number, anyway. The voice was mildly familiar.

"Is that the editor?" she asked.

"One of them. What's up?"

Who . . .

"This is Queenie Hart," she said.

"Ah! The Queen of Tarts."

"That's right. A copy of *Stradevarious* was on my step this morning."

"The *Strad* gets about. By the way, this is Bernie Tucker. I was at your place last week."

"Yes . . . and thanks for getting Nona to help me out last Saturday. I appreciated it."

"No worries. What can I do for you, Queenie? Got something you want to put in the *Strad*?"

"Not today—though thanks for the advert, and I will advertise when I get organised. What I wanted is some information on The Belfry."

"Not a lot I can tell you. As we said, it was a church when Maur and I were kids, but when the old minister died, the parish had trouble getting anyone to come here. Congregations were shrinking, and in the end, everyone just went to the church at Borrow. The old rectory wasn't too sound, so when a tree fell through the roof sometime in the early seventies, the site was cleared.

"The church was deconsecrated and sold off to an out-of-town couple. They lived there for a bit and then—" He broke off. "I don't know if this is the stuff you want to know?"

"I was hoping there might be some history to it," Queenie said, half-truthfully. She was really hoping there wasn't.

"Ah—well I'm sure we did a piece in the *Strad* for the sesquicentenary back in the late nineties. I can get Maur to look it out for you."

"That would be good, if it's not too much trouble."

"Maur won't mind. She's the history buff. She's digitalised the earlier editions, and we have an online edition too." He sounded proud of the fact.

"Thank you," Queenie said.

She felt somewhat less apprehensive. If The Belfry had been notorious, then Bernie would have known about it.

"I'll have her email you the link," Bernie said. He wished her well and then he ended the call.

Queenie's admiration for the couple grew.

Unfortunately, the short conversation wasn't enough to distract her from the weirdness of having the lease papers vanish from under her hand.

Chapter Fifteen: Oliver

Queenie Hart. September, 2021

Queenie wanted to call Andy, Branok, or the Fixer. She wasn't sure which, so instead she headed out for a walk.

The no-boomerang arrangement she had with her parents meant she had known for years that she had to rely upon herself to sort out the challenges of life. Since finding herself cornered by the chicken-and-egg of Queen of Tarts and Angel Petty, she'd had to rely on Branok, then on Andy and now on the Fixer for help and for information.

They had all come through for her, but she had to take back the power of autonomy. They owed her nothing, and she had annoyed them all, often intentionally. She had less than a month until the Caledonian Curse struck, and she would begin to annoy people without conscious intention. Once *that* was underway, she'd have to avoid company as much as she could, so she needed to butter bread *now,* to buy some prepaid goodwill and forgiveness.

She'd better advertise in the *Strad* to explain she wouldn't be at the market for the month of October.

She'd also need a safe no-contact place for folk to collect orders from The Belfry.

Her walk took her around the old graveyard. That might have seemed morbid to her in the Mother Goose Lane days, but in the fresh air of Kirk Circle, it seemed reasonable.

Getting to know the neighbours in case I abuse them next month.

The old trees were dark and forbidding, but once out in the

sunshine of early spring, she found the graveyard unexpectedly soothing and even entertaining.

The stones had mellowed. Some of the graves dwelled within low iron railings. Some had cracked concrete counterpanes rimmed with moss, and there were others with permanent stone vases bearing the remnants of long-ago floral tributes.

Flowers planted decades ago had naturalised themselves in the short, coarse grass. Probably someone mowed it sometimes, although piles of small droppings suggested kangaroos and rabbits grazed there, too.

Queenie set herself to getting familiar with the long-gone tenants. She found some Tuckers, who were probably Bernie's ancestors. Other surnames recurred too, but she wasn't familiar enough with Fiddle Bay to recognise many. Nona's married name was Tilbury, and there were six of those.

She looked for Mitchells but found none. That wasn't conclusive. The Fixer could have come from anywhere. She had no idea where he lived.

You know his name. One of them.

Ah! The smugness of private knowledge.

There were three vicars buried in the graveyard, close together, so perhaps they liked the company. The dates seemed too long ago for any of them to be the one the Tuckers remembered, but Queenie was glad they were there.

I could come and Confess to them, if I ever felt the need.

The place was quiet, breezy, and charming in its way. It wasn't sad or creepy. It was a celebration of other folk who'd known the refuge of Fiddle Bay.

Queenie returned to The Belfry in a happier mood. Maybe Maureen Tucker had sent her the promised link already.

She knew it was unlikely, but anyway, she could do a *check-me-out* search for The Belfry. She should have done that before. If there was anything spooky about the old ex-church, *someone* would have spread the news.

She mounted the steps to the foyer and stepped through the inner arch. She hadn't bothered to lock up. Few people came to the end of October Road, and anyway, she'd been just a little way back in the graveyard.

She paused on her way to the kitchen to snag the *Stradevarious* from the table in the main room. She might find something interesting in the articles. There was one on the Oakengrove Experience that she hadn't finished yet.

She was in the act of tucking it under her arm when a large yellow envelope materialised on the table.

Queenie stifled a squeal of shock.

She stared at the thing. If she'd come in from her walk just five minutes later—three minutes, even—the envelope would have been there already, and she'd have thought she was going mad.

Maybe I am.

She reached out and dabbed her fingertips on the envelope quickly, as if it might be hot.

It did feel mildly warm, as if it had been resting in the sun.

Holding her breath, she picked it up.

She noticed it was the same envelope, but when she turned it over, she saw the seal had been broken. It was now fastened down with a blob of wax stamped with a monogram. *PO* or *OP*.

She took it to the kitchen, where she put the jug on to boil, then peeled off the wax, opened the flap, and extracted the papers.

It was the lease, of course. What else had she expected?

There were her initials on the first page. Next to them was another set, penned with what was surely an old-fashioned dip pen. *OP,* like the wax seal, she thought, although the letters were entwined, so it was difficult to be sure which came first.

She flipped back to the last page, where she saw her own signature, along with the name of the witness, and a matching pair of names for the other party to the deal.

Oliver Porthwellian. The witness was *A. Tredennick.* She should have expected that.

She turned her attention to the Fixer's contribution.

MJS K*squiggle.*

"Not helpful," she said aloud. She squinted at the printed name. *Mitchell Kingsolver.*

Mitchell. First name, then.

Kingsolver. Really?

Mitchell Kingsolver. *Yes*! She punched the air.

I know something you don't know I know. Na-na-na na-na!

She sighed at her own ridiculousness.

Idiot. You had only to ask him. You've addressed him as Mitch, *so he probably thinks you knew his name already. He probably never even thought of introducing himself conventionally.*

Mitchell Kingsolver.

She liked the name. She liked *him*, she supposed, insofar as she could like someone whose face she couldn't bring to mind.

She remembered his hands. He'd used one to steady the lease and the other to use the pen. Nice hands. Capable.

She thought of his various caps, and she tried to remember the rest of his clothing. It must be something entirely ordinary. *He* must be entirely ordinary. He probably looked like one of those actors with the mid-brown hair and the pleasant blunt faces who popped up as neighbours and best friends and gardeners and tradies in a hundred forgettable TV series and ads for plumbers. You always knew you'd seen them in something, but you could never remember what. If you thought you knew and looked up the cast of a movie, you found out it wasn't the one you were thinking of, but a look-alike.

Mitchell Kingsolver. I'm so *going to take your photo the next time I see you.*

Better yet, she could look him up on *check-me-out* now that she had his name. His first name was common, but his surname wasn't. She didn't think she'd ever met anyone else with it.

Or else they're all as forgettable as this one.

If he's so forgettable, why are you obsessing about him?

She laid down the lease agreement with a sigh. All this faffing about was a mental smokescreen to divert her attention from the real puzzle.

The envelope had vanished from under her fingers. An hour or so later, it had reappeared in the same manner, countersigned, witnessed, and sealed. No one had fetched it—at least, not physically—and no one had returned it.

Oliver Porthwellian, ninety-six years old and disliking mobile phones and meter boxes, could somehow conjure papers about without touching them.

Well, Andy had said something about conjuring. He must have meant it in a literal manner.

No ghosts, then. Nothing to fear. The Belfry wasn't haunted. It was just an old man . . . an old fairy man . . . playing about and depriving the postal service of its just revenue.

Queenie tucked the lease agreement into the top shelf of the bookcase in the main room. She didn't want it in her bedroom in case Oliver Porthwellian's talents extended to invisible prowling.

The idea of a nonagenarian invisible-prowling wasn't all that scary, but she'd rather he went rummaging in the bookshelf than anywhere else.

That was idiotic. How would he know where she'd stashed it?

She called Andy Tredennick.

"Porthwellian and Tredennick. Androw—"

"Hi, Andy."

"Hello—Queenie."

"Got it in one." She beamed at the ceiling, imagining his face with its fine lines and lovely mouth.

"You're the only caller who interrupts me before I get my opening salvo out," he said.

"Okay. Sorry."

"You don't sound sorry."

"Not sorry, then. Andy, I got the lease back."

"O-kaaay?" He sounded puzzled.

"I saw it come back."

"Oh."

"Poof."

"I seriously doubt that."

"No, it just did a now-you-don't-see-it-now-you-do."

"I see."

"Did Oliver conjure it back to the table, or is he rambling around in here being invisible?"

"He's not there," Andy said.

"Are you sure? I'm about to have a bath and I'd hate to give the old gentleman a heart attack."

There was a short pause and then a deep, cultured voice said, "I can assure you I'm not there, Miss Hart. I'm here. And if I were there, I would not have a heart attack at the sight of a miss in a state of glorious nature. My heart will wear out sooner rather than later, but it won't have an attack. It will just wind down and stop. I'll have fair warning, but I'm assured it won't be unpleasant."

Queenie had no ready retort to that, so she just said lamely, "Not the invisible man, then."

"Not even a little bit. Tell me, do you like my old home?"

Queenie let this sink in and realised she wasn't surprised. "You lived here?"

"For a time, back in the day. However, the walk to the office became arduous, so I relinquished The Belfry into the firm's gift. I quite love the place, you see, and I wanted to have some say in what quality of person was allowed to live there."

"I see."

"My junior partner assures me you are suitable *pro tem,* and that you are comely and industrious."

"I bake," Queenie agreed. She didn't feel qualified to judge on what an old fairy man might mean by *comely.*

"It has been suggested one should sample the quality before endorsing a talent."

"He means sample the baking," Dellion's distant voice qualified.

"Okay. If you're ever this way, let me know and I'll give you some tarts to sample. Or—" She had an inspiration. "If I set a box of tarts on the table where the lease was, would you be able to get them?"

"I would, if you put them in the large Cornfellow tureen rather than a box."

Queenie was unsure what a tureen was, but fortunately, Dellion piped up from where she was doubtless enjoying the exchange to inform her it was a *kind of covered bowl with a fancy lid.*

"The one with the lacy black leaf pattern?" Queenie suggested.

There was a thoughtful silence from Oliver.

"It might not be leaves, exactly . . ."

"It's Cornfellow ware—stamped on the base," Dellion said, after a muttered consultation.

"Okay. That one." She'd look up the provenance later.

"Was that all?" Andy asked after a moment.

"Oh—yes, I suppose so."

"Good. Goodb—"

Oliver interrupted quickly. "When may I collect my tarts, Miss Hart?"

Queenie heard a note of urgency in his voice.

"I expect you'd like them fresh rather than frozen, so shall we say . . . oh, in about three hours?"

"Excellent," Oliver said. He added, "At my age one doesn't wish to wait too long for the important things."

Queenie wondered why, in that case, he'd left it so long to fetch the lease agreement. She didn't say so. She had an oven to heat, tarts to construct, and a tureen to track down . . .and she'd given herself the bare minimum time to do it.

Pride and vainglory go before a fall.

Check-me-out had nothing to say about Cornfellow ware, so Queenie began mixing and rolling and then fell to examining the crockery while the pastry rested. She turned one of the black-patterned cups upside down and identified the mark Dellion had mentioned.

This made it easy enough to track down the large tureen, an elegant boat-shaped bowl with elongated handles and a lid. It was the biggest of three similar ones in different patterns . . . big enough to require both hands and some effort to lift.

She rolled out, formed and filled the tarts with more than usual care. She had no doubt Oliver had high standards. Old he was, but he had strong opinions and an articulate way of stating them. He evidently wasn't the sort of elder who liked to stick with the bland and familiar.

She lined the tureen with greaseproof paper, removed the tarts from the oven, and set them to cool.

With the time moving faster than she liked, she packed the still-slightly-warm tarts into the tureen in layers, with paper in between.

I shouldn't promise what I can't deliver . . . I ought to have made shortcrust . . . I ought to have told him tomorrow. *I was showing off.*

Still, sometimes pride in one's work was pardonable. With one minute to spare, she set the tureen on the table where the envelope had been.

Then, naturally, she sat down with her elbows on the table and her chin in her hands and stared fixedly at the tureen while she counted down the seconds.

She was morally certain Oliver Porthwellian would be

counting down as well.

I wonder what happens if you photograph something vanish –

The tureen was gone.

Chapter Sixteen: Tea and Tarts

Queenie Hart. September, 2021

Seeing the tureen vanish left Queenie almost as much in the dark as ever, but at least she could assure herself that vanishing and appearing items were a *thing* rather than a slip of sanity.

The tureen reappeared a couple of days after it vanished. This time Queenie wasn't there to see it appear, but she found it early in the morning.

She opened the lid with mild trepidation. The tarts had gone, and the tureen was clean and dry. Inside was a folded sheet of high-quality paper bearing the letterhead of Porthwellian Tredennick.

Queenie unfolded it to reveal a handwritten order for a dozen assorted tarts to be delivered weekly on Sundays *until somebody informs you I no longer have need of them, or I decide to change the quantity. Please include your nominated price which I shall remit each week until or unless the price rises, in which case you will inform me of the new arrangement, and I shall remit that amount instead.* He was *yours sincerely, Oliver Porthwellian.*

"Well!" Queenie said aloud.

Obviously, Oliver had enjoyed her gift and decided to endorse her talents . . .in baking, at least.

Market day was approaching, and again she faced the problem of finding transport.

Reluctantly, she telephoned the Fixer.

It wasn't that she didn't want to see him again—she did, if only to get a fix on his face—but she was still not pleased to be dependent on other people, even though she was paying him.

"Fixer," his familiar voice said, as it had the first time.

Queenie said, "Hello, Mitch."

"Hello," he said unhelpfully.

"This is Queenie Hart. Queen of Tarts."

"I've been hoping you'd call," he said. "I want more tarts. Lots more tarts. A great many tarts."

"I'll be at the market on Saturday . . . if I can get there."

"I'll take you," he said immediately.

This time, she didn't refuse the offer. "Okay, thank you."

"I'll pick you up at about six," he said.

"Did you—"

"Do you—"

They spoke in chorus and broke off.

"Go ahead," the Fixer said.

"Did you get a chance to ask your cousin about the tricycle?"

"Georgiana said you're welcome to it, but it's not as big as I remembered. It wouldn't be practical in bad weather."

"I'd still like to try it out," she said.

"I'll bring it over on Sunday."

"Thanks."

There was an awkward pause.

"Mitch? What were you about to say, before?"

"I was about to ask if you still wanted the tricycle, but we've covered that."

"Okay. I'll see you on Saturday morning. How many tarts do you want, and what sort?"

"I'll buy them at the market," he said. He added, "See you Saturday."

Queenie ended the call, more disconcerted than ever.

His voice was familiar, and she could picture his lanky frame, probably leaning on something as he spoke into the phone. She remembered his dependable hands, with their short, neat nails and broad thumbs.

She spoke into the dead air of the ended call. "Mitchell Kingsolver, you *will* see me Saturday. And I will see *you* on Saturday and take notice of your face. You may depend on it."

Assured of transport, for at least that week, she baked a great many tarts.

By Friday night, The Belfry was redolent of jam, jelly, syrup and custard-filled shortcrust and puff pastry, and Queenie had run out of boxes.

On Saturday morning, just before six, she heard the quiet whirr of an engine and the faint swish of tyres.

She was already dressed and ready, and she hurried to the foyer as soon as the Fixer tapped on the door.

She had the door open almost instantly, but he had already stepped back, and half turned away.

"If you put the boxes on the step, I can stow them in the bus."

"Good morning to you, too," Queenie said to the back of his head.

She carried the boxes as he asked and then she rushed back in for her signs and order forms, cards, and brochures.

He took them from her and gestured to the bus with a jerk of his head. "Hop in."

She hopped in.

A few seconds later he did too, straight to the driver's seat. He started the engine.

"Where did you put—" She broke off.

"Your signs and things are in the back." His voice was muffled as he pulled around the wall and headed out on October Road.

"Have you got a sore throat, or are you chewing something?" Queenie asked.

He swallowed. "I liberated a box of Ruby Tuesday. I hope you don't mind. I do intend to pay for them."

"And I do intend to pay for the ride," Queenie said.

"Shall we call it even? I'll still buy some more when we get there."

"Fine. I'm sorry you had to get up so early."

"I don't mind. I told you, I like to fix things."

Queenie watched the empty fields and saw Oakengrove, the big house, coming into sight. "I managed to get a stall at the Oakengrove Festival."

He said, "Are you serving tea too?"

"What? Why?"

"Tea and tarts. You could offer afternoon tea."

"So I could, but it's too late to organise this time. I'm surprised they let me have a stall, considering it's so close."

"Next year," he said.

"If I'm still here."

He turned to look at her, his face in shadow. "Where else would you be?"

That was the question.

She said, "Mitch, I have The Belfry for three months. I can extend the time after that if I choose."

"Will you?"

"At this stage, I hope so and I expect so. It depends on whether I can make a good enough living to stay here once the three months is up."

Once the rent kicks in . . . however much it is.

They'd reached the green, where stalls were setting up. Nona wasn't there this week, but Maureen Tucker was.

She beckoned to Queenie as soon as she was out of the bus. "You're on stall 16B this time, Queenie," she said.

Queenie thanked her. She was about to start unloading when Maureen held out a hand. "Bernie said you were interested in the history of your belfry. If you've got a minute, I'll give you a magazine. I was going to send a link, but I got side-tracked."

Queenie remembered, with surprise, that she'd intended to pursue the matter on *check-me-out.* She hadn't got far, and then she'd learned that Oliver Porthwellian had once lived there, the problem of the vanishing and reappearing envelope had been cleared up, and the urgency to learn more had receded.

Still, she thanked Maureen, and went with her to an onsite van, where she received a vintage copy of *The Stradevarious.*

Turning back to her stall, she discovered it all set up, with everything in place.

The Fixer—Mitchell Kingsolver—must indeed move like lightning.

She looked for him, but he'd gone, along with the green bus. She went to put the float in her cashbox and found it already contained a selection of notes. A slip of paper stated that the money was to pay for the tarts, less the box of Ruby Tuesdays, as agreed.

Queenie checked her set-up and she calculated that two dozen assorted tarts and an extra box of Ruby Tuesdays had disappeared.

That reminded her that she needed to prepare Oliver Porthwellian's weekly order upon her return, and park it on the table.

She shook her head. Her life was becoming steadily more bizarre . . . and the Caledonian Curse hadn't even arrived yet!

Sales that day went as briskly as they had the first week, and a gratifying number of her original patrons returned for more. Queenie sold out by two o'clock, but she stayed on for a while, as a few orders for the week after came in.

She explained that next week was fine, but the one after she'd be at Oakengrove. That turned out not to be a problem, as the market was relocating there anyway on the grounds that most of the village would be going to the festival.

Maureen Tucker returned at three. "All done, Queenie?"

She nodded. "Thanks for the magazine. I haven't read it yet, but I certainly will."

Maureen smiled. "I re-read the Belfry article and I think you'll find it helpful. There's not a lot about it in recent years, but the decades when it was a working church are covered.

"A chap named Porthwellian bought it and did the conversion himself. Miffed some of the local tradies. He wasn't the sociable kind, which was why Bernie and I were glad to have a look inside when you came. He left some years back, and since then people have come and gone. Not sure who owns it now."

The slightest uptilt in her voice told Queenie she wasn't the only person fishing for information. She saw no harm in explaining.

"I'm not sure who the legal owner is, but it's administered by a company called Porthwellian Tredennick, in Victoria."

"Still connected to Mister Porthwellian, then," Maureen said. She smiled, and added, "You shouldn't have much trouble with the landlord dropping by unannounced if they're in Victoria."

Queenie agreed. *You don't know the half of it.*

"Are you all right to get home?" Maureen asked.

"I believe so. Mitch brought me in the bus, and he'll take me back. I think."

She frowned, recalling she hadn't thanked him for the ride that morning.

"Well, if you—" Maureen looked over her shoulder. "No, here he is now."

Queenie wanted to ask the knowledgeable Missus Tucker about Mitch, but she thought it might look odd, or particular, or something.

She stacked up her materials and turned to watch the bus pulling into a parking space next to the green.

"Since you're okay, I'll be off," Maureen said.

Queenie turned to say goodbye and bent to retrieve her belongings.

They were gone.

Mister Lightning Octopus Mitchell the Fixer Kingsolver had appropriated them already.

Queenie got in the bus as Mitch sprang in the other side.

"I didn't know if you'd come," she said.

"I'll always come if you want me."

"Yes, but we'd arranged that you'd bring me here. We didn't discuss going back."

"You can walk, if you prefer. It's no distance, but I thought you wouldn't want to carry all these things."

"I don't! I'm grateful you came."

He pulled away from the parking space. "Cup of coffee?"

"Er—" Queenie was tired of second-guessing him, so she said, "Are you asking if I'll make you one, or are you inviting me to come for one with you?"

"I thought we had a raincheck."

"Oh."

"Ask or invite . . . Does it matter?"

"Not really." She added in a burst, "The answer's the same in either case."

He didn't reply, so she asked, "My place or a café?"

"Maybe your place. I can help you to unload."

She nodded. He'd been in The Belfry already, so once more wasn't going to be a problem.

She let herself in and left him to bring in the boxes, since she knew he'd do it anyway.

"Tea or coffee?" she called as she heard him come in. And then she felt ridiculous because he'd asked for coffee.

"Tea," he said.

"Tart?"

"Yes. In plural."

More tarts? He ought to be the size of a house!

She made tea and offered him a mug and a couple of experimental tarts that hadn't made the cut for the market.

"What are these?"

"Undecided or maybe Gender Fluids," she said.

He looked down at the custard filling, criss-crossed blue from blueberry juice and pink from cochineal and he laughed.

He had a pleasant laugh, and Queenie smiled.

"Mitch."

"Yes?" he said through a mouthful.

"Do you mind if I take your picture?"

That seemed to surprise him, but after a moment, he said, "Why do you want to do that?"

She said, awkwardly, "For some reason, I have trouble recalling your face."

"Oh. Does that matter?"

"Not really, I suppose."

"Hm."

"I don't mean to be rude."

He tilted a quick grin at her. "You're not, usually. Although you *can* be quite startlingly rude on occasion, you don't like upsetting people unintentionally, right?"

"I don't, usually."

"That landlady of yours—you wouldn't have minded upsetting her."

"No. She upset *me*."

"Want me to put a hex on her for you?"

She stared at him in shock. "No!" Then she added, "Could you?"

He shrugged. "I'm not sure, love. If you badly wanted me to, and if you asked me to, I'd probably try."

"Don't."

"All right. Probably as well."

He clasped his hands and went off into his thoughts, absently rubbing one thumb against the other wrist.

Queenie reached out and put her hand on his. His skin was warm and surprisingly soft. "Have you got a sore hand?"

"No."

"Nervous tic?"

"Not that I know of. Why?"

"You were rubbing your wrist."

"Was I?" He looked down at her hand on his and twisted around so he was holding hers. "You have nice generous hands, Queenie Hart. Strong, with soft skin."

She said, uncomfortably, "That's from handling pastry. Butter and sugar are an old folk remedy for rough skin."

He nodded, still looking down at their hands. "Would you really have come out for a drink with me this time?"

"We are having a drink," she reminded.

"So we are, but it's not a *date,* is it?"

"No. It's me getting you a cup of tea because you wanted one and because it's the right thing to do. You've done such a lot to help me."

"It's not altruism."

"I know. You're a fixer."

"That's what I am."

"May I have a photograph then?"

He looked up. "As long as you don't intend to use it for nefarious purposes."

"I won't. I said no to the hex, remember?"

"What *will* you do with it? Sleep with it under your pillow? I believe that's a folk remedy for something or other."

"Hardly, since it will be in my phone."

"You can have your picture—tomorrow."

"Why tomorrow?"

"Because I want to find something out from you—tomorrow. Nothing bad." He gave her hand a squeeze, let go, and got to his feet. "Goodbye, Queenie. I'll bring the tricycle tomorrow, so you can have it for next week's market.

"By the way, if you could have picked one of the names your parents almost used for you, which would you have taken?"

About to give her stock answer, that she didn't know and couldn't choose, any more than her parents had been able to, she stopped short, frowning. "I never told you about my name."

"Yes you did. You said you were Queenie Hart. *I* never told you mine, but you know it."

"Mitch. I heard the bus passengers use it."

"Do you know the rest of it?"

"I do. Mitchell Kingsolver."

"How do you know? You've never heard the bus passengers call me that. I doubt if they even know I have a last name. They just think of me as *Mitch the driver*."

"You witnessed my signature on the lease agreement, and you printed your name."

He smiled. "So you see . . . we find names out in all sorts of ways. I'll see you tomorrow."

He left, then, and Queenie was too bothered to say goodbye.

Chapter Seventeen: Snapshots

Queenie Hart. September, 2021

Queenie put together Oliver Porthwellian's weekly order of tarts. Then she read the vintage issue of *The Stradevarious* that Maureen Tucker had given her.

It was interesting, especially the old photos showing the church with its then vicar. She learned some of the church-specific names for architecture that she hadn't known before. The little porch she'd been thinking of as the foyer was in fact a narthex. Apart from that, the article didn't tell her much to explain the place as it was now, but she'd concluded the oddness she'd been seeing was entirely down to Oliver's skill in bypassing the laws of physics to shift things about without being present to touch them.

The vanishing and appearing items were the *only* oddities really, aside from the doubts other people had expressed about her new home.

So the last two or three tenants hadn't stayed long. Maybe they found it too isolated, or they didn't fancy living near a graveyard. Maybe they hadn't come up to Oliver's stringent expectations. If they didn't, he was more than capable of getting rid of them. She absolved him of invisible prowling, but that didn't mean he wouldn't, and hadn't, set out to arrange a few little off-putting surprises. Having things appear and vanish would do it.

She hoped he enjoyed his tarts enough to give her a tick of approval to last beyond her three months.

She wondered if Branok and Gillan St Ives knew Oliver. Maybe that had been why Branok had sounded doubtful about recommending her for The Belfry.

Unable to settle, she walked out to the graveyard and leaned against the sun-warmed wall near the place she thought of as *Vicar-ville.* She had a brief and frank conversation with the vicars, explaining a few things she didn't want to tell the living.

When she felt more settled, she said, "Thanks . . . and don't worry. I'm going to care for your old church. I might do some Belfry Special tarts, with little crosses on them. They'd be nice for Easter if I'm still here."

The departed vicars didn't answer, of course, but she felt comforted anyway.

She hoped they had been nice men, broad-minded and forgiving. She also hoped they wouldn't mind their church being turned into a sort of factory for tarts.

She returned to The Belfry and occupied herself with an inventory of the stores she'd need from Fiddle-de-Dee for the upcoming festival. It was two full days, so did that mean she'd need to make four times as many tarts?

I'll need more boxes.

On Sunday morning, Oliver's order had vanished from the table. A few hours later, the money, in cash, appeared in the returned tureen. To Queenie's mingled amusement and astonishment Oliver had taken it upon himself to review the tarts, awarding them points out of ten.

He wrote that he had not as yet eaten them all, but he had cut a sample of each style and judged it aesthetically, and then by texture, flavour, smell, and satisfaction. He rather thought he'd have more of the Raspberry Relish in his next order. He also asked if she made currant tarts and if not, why not.

Queenie thought she'd have to invent a few more styles to keep him entertained.

She was busy making notes of possible flavour

combinations when she heard the bus arrive.

She sprang to her feet, almost knocking the laptop askew in her hurry.

He's late . . . where has he . . . oh, the bus timetable! He must have had passengers to take to the big house.

She was heading for the door when her phone rang.

She almost hit *decline,* but at this stage she couldn't afford to miss orders or to offend customers.

She accepted the call. "Hello—"

"Hello, Queenie."

It was the Fixer.

She said, blankly, "But you're just outside, aren't you?"

"That's right. I told you I needed some information today."

"All right. What?"

He asked, "What do I look like?"

"I—I *told* you. I can't remember!"

"Just think—no, don't open the door. It won't do you any good because you can't see my face even if you do. What do I look like?"

She sighed. "Tallish. Taller than me, anyway. Is that right?"

"Yes. What else?"

She tried to focus on impressions. "You have good hands. Broad, with nice warm skin. Not chilly or sticky or clammy or rough."

"Okay. Next?"

"You're not as heavy as you ought to be, considering the amount you eat. Must be all that hopping in and out of the bus. You wear caps most of the time. Big ones, with logos, according to whatever job you're doing."

"And my face?"

"That's all. Sorry."

"We've established that you have at least an impression of me as I am now. Do you always have problems recalling faces?"

"Not usually," she said with growing discomfort.

Not ever, apart from his.

"Must be something or other I did or said in the beginning." He didn't sound too bothered.

"I don't understand."

"I'll have to give it some thought."

"You do that. May I open the door now?"

"It's your door, so of course you can open it." He sounded surprised.

Queenie glanced at the belltower door with the looped rope handle. She still hadn't got that open.

"Can I still have that picture?"

"If you want."

She opened the door and peered out. He was standing with his back to her.

Didn't trust me not to peep.

"Mitch?"

He turned to face her, and he slowly took off his busman's cap.

"Hello, Queenie Hart. How will you have me?"

She stared at him in perplexity. It had to be him. It was obviously, definitely, indisputably, him. It was the bus driver, the Fixer, and Mitchell Kingsolver, who had given her help far beyond what she'd hired him to do. Nevertheless, the face wasn't the one she would have pictured for him if she'd been able to picture one. She'd been thinking *ordinary,* and *forgettable,* but it wasn't.

He was highly memorable.

He came over and reached for her hand. "Don't look so worried, love. When you're meant to see me properly, you will. Maybe in November." She held her breath, but he just took the phone from her loosened grasp and peered at it.

She remembered him fiddling with his phone when she was attempting to pay him for bringing her and her chattels to The Belfry.

"You're not very good with those, are you, Mitch."

He chuckled. "Not especially, but I think I can get this one to take a photo if I push enough buttons."

"I'm the one who wants the photo," she reminded.

He handed over the phone. "All set up, I think."

He took out his own and poked a few keys in a hopeful but clueless manner.

"Mitch!"

He looked up from fiddling with his phone.

She snapped the photo.

"Queenie!"

"What?"

She shied. He'd snapped her back.

"Fair is fair. If you get one of me, then I deserve one of you."

She couldn't argue with that.

He tucked the phone back into his pocket, without offering her a chance to approve the image.

She wondered if she should lead by example, and show him what she'd got, but what if he hated it? She'd have to delete it and she wasn't going to give up her photograph. Superstitiously, she hadn't even looked at it yet. It was a treasure to be checked later.

"I have the tricycle," Mitch said, gesturing at the bus. As far as she could tell, he hadn't looked at what he had, either.

He's so inept he probably got a blurry shot of my ear and one elbow.

"I have something of yours, too," Queenie said, remembering.

"Tarts?"

"You have tarts on the brain." She dashed inside and fetched the pen from the table where it had been since she removed it from the envelope.

She returned to offer it to him and discovered that of course he'd already unloaded the tricycle.

"You left this behind when you witnessed my signature. It

was clipped to the envelope, and I didn't even notice when I put it to be collected," she said.

He nodded his thanks and hooked the pen to an inside pocket. At least, she supposed he had. She hoped it didn't leak.

The tricycle was large and sturdy, and it was painted in a jumble of bright colours.

"Georgiana wanted to be visible to oncoming traffic on dull days," Mitch said. He added, "She said you can repaint it if you want. The trailer is well sprung, and it has good tyres. I checked the pressure and the integrity."

They contemplated the vehicle for a minute or so.

"Are you going to try it?" Mitch asked.

"Yes, but not now with you watching. It's been too long."

He nodded his understanding. "I'll get going then. Just one thing, Queenie. I don't think this will carry all the boxes you'll need at the Oakengrove Experience, and traffic may be heavy. Shall I pick you up on the Saturday? I assume you'll be going home on the night, and then coming back for the Sunday. I could do all four trips if you can be a wee bit flexible with the timing. I'll be driving practically all day anyway."

"The festival's that big a deal?"

"Big enough," he said. "It's a major money spinner for the bay, and a fine showcase for indie bands. Some quite big names still play here because this is where they got their start."

"Who?"

"Fusilier, Esperanto's Baby—oh, and Courtesan."

"Thank you then," she said, unwilling to admit she knew none of these bands. "That is, I'll agree to the Saturday and then see what happens. I may not do both days."

"I should think both days would be a good idea, because word of mouth is your friend, and sweet things often sneak into your psyche and tempt you to a return bout," he said.

He left then, and Queenie, as so often after an encounter with Mitch Kingsolver, was left perplexed.

I should have invited him to stay for a drink, at least.

"Oh!" She'd just remembered she had to make an order at Fiddle-de-Dee, but that would have to wait a day or two now. She couldn't expect Mitch to drive out to The Belfry yet again.

Chapter Eighteen: Housewarming Gift

Queenie Hart. September, 2021

Not long before the festival at Oakengrove, a large package appeared on Queenie's doorstep. This time, it came via normal postal delivery and, as the package was dropped off by a young woman on a postie bike, Queenie was sure it wasn't Mitch.

She took the parcel in and was pleased to see it came from a bookshop called The Orange Grove. The name summoned the vision of a warm place full of scents, and sunshine, and she was disposed to like the book even before she carried it into the main room and unwrapped it.

Once the paper was off, the book was further enclosed in a drawstring bag of soft material so silky Queenie couldn't be sure whether it was paper or cloth.

She slid it out and discovered why it merited such careful packaging.

It was a slipcase figured in gold and green, and engraved with a title—*Orders of the Fay*. The author's name was Piers le Fay, and the illustrator was Pen Inkersoll.

Queenie turned the slipcase sideways and five beautiful books slid out. They fitted loosely and she realised there should have been more. She examined the titles.

1. *Alpenfolk, Braefolk and Courtfolk*
2. *Delftvolk, Elves, Fijordfee, and Fisherfolk*
3. *Galleonfee, Herdfee, Hobs, and Kanalfee*

4. *Leprechauns, Piskies, and Pixies*
7. *The Fay Companion.*

An embossed certificate accompanied the collection, and also a printed note on bookshop paper.

The Orange Grove

Dear Queenie,

This set of books comes to you as a housewarming gift from the folk at Porthwellian Tredennick. *They asked us to send you the deluxe edition of this work, although it is currently incomplete. You'll observe books 5 and 6 are not included. They will be despatched as soon as we receive the stock from the printer.*

We hope you enjoy your gift. This series has been quite popular although reviewers seem unable to place it neatly within a genre.

All the best,

Jonquil Lemon Orange – yes, that really is my name.

Queenie opened the first book and read the introduction. She could see why reviewers might find it difficult to place.

On the face of it, it was an anthropological treatise of various peoples, discussing their history, culture, and social structure, touching on clothing, recreation, and traditional foods.

On the other hand, the peoples were different orders of the fay, so many readers would suppose the works were fantasy mocumentaries . . . if such a genre existed.

It was a literary curiosity, but she remembered Andy telling her that her housewarming present would explain about conjuring.

Now she saw what he meant.

She already had some grasp of it, from seeing what Oliver could do, but she still didn't know what was meant by *getting a fix* or why he was the only one who could do it. Something about being the only one who had been to The Belfry – and indeed he had lived there for a time.

She glanced through the first few entries, stopping now

and again to read a passage. Conjuring was mentioned, but not described in detail. It was as if the author wrote for an audience already *au fait* with the term.

Maybe that was so.

Queenie laid aside the first book and picked up the one that was out of sequence.

She saw at once that this was the one for her purpose.

The Fay Companion, instead of being a description of a particular order of people, turned out to be an encyclopaedia of terms and concepts common to many, if not all the orders.

Queenie supposed it made sense, because it would save the author and readers from re-treading the same ground in different books in the set.

She turned to the entries for C and found *Conjuring*. It was one of the longer entries, but she read it in full. When she'd finished, she sat thoughtfully for a while, matching up details she'd read with her observations and things Andy had said.

The reason Oliver could conjure items to and from The Belfry amounted to his ability to get a mental fix—which seemed to mean he could see in his mind's eye exactly where something would be. The papers had appeared on a table that no doubt dated from his tenure. They were in an envelope he could easily visualise because he'd chosen it, and they had left in the same way. The tarts travelled in a tureen he knew well, from that same table. She'd offered to put them in a box, but the old man would not have been able to visualise that, because he wouldn't know the size, shape, colour or even the material.

After reading the entry she even knew, or suspected, why there had been a delay in the papers being *snagged*.

Apparently, items could be conjured within narrow parameters. The item had to belong to the person conjuring it or be something he or she had every right to take. It had to be something that could be got by other, more ordinary means, it had to be inanimate or at the very least non-sentient, and it had to be something to fetch or send at a precise and easily visualised location.

Mitch had witnessed her signature on the lease and had then absentmindedly clipped his pen to the envelope. Maybe that pen, which didn't belong to Oliver and which he had no right to remove, had prevented him from taking the envelope.

Queenie felt mildly smug about having worked that out, although she didn't know if her reasoning was correct.

She read the next few entries and learned about *courting cake, the courtlands, colouring up* and *cuddling chairs*. Next came *danz damar, dirndls* and *disclosure.*

She paused there, remembering the term Branok and Gill and Andy had used for the Caledonian Curse.

Manifestation, or *mani.* She turned to the middle of the book, and there it was. She read the definition more than once, but it was necessarily vague. The author said it was impossible to cover all manifestations, because there were so many and new ones could pop up at any time and create their own set of rules. He further claimed that even the fay themselves weren't sure what they were.

One theory claims the mani or mani-self is a version of the person it affects as he or she might have been in centuries past.

Queenie scowled at this. "Does that mean I was a bad-tempered, abusive Scotswoman a few hundred years ago? Or is it more that if I'd been born then instead of in the 1990s, I'd have grown into a bad-tempered, abusive Scotswoman with a besom? How bizarre."

She reread the other theories. One suggested the mani-self was the fay person in his or her purest form—*the most himself he will ever be.*

"Lawks, I hope not!"

Another one stated that the manifestation might be a secondary personality which was able to take form within or sometimes around the host, effectively pushing the everyday persona into a dreamlike or distant state where he was aware of the manifestation's actions and words, but was unable or insufficiently motivated to intervene.

Yet another mentioned mani personalities where the host changed and became unrecognisable, appearing as someone else.

This variation runs in families, although not every child in such a family is identically affected. Other than that, no one has been able to identify the gene responsible.

"Hmph," Queenie said. She wanted to get her hands on the author and pry a definite opinion out of him.

All this—some say, others believe, it is suggested, it may be that—it's all maddening. How can you be an expert and not *know what it is?*

It came to her that she'd never known what the Caledonian Curse was, and she should be an accredited expert on that.

She called Andy.

"Porth—"

"Cut the shite, Andy."

She heard a softly uttered *oh, dear,* and then Andy said, "Good morning, Queenie."

She growled at him.

"What's wrong?" He sounded apprehensive and surprised.

Queenie breathed in deeply. "It's all verra fine—" She stopped, hearing the dreaded dialect creeping into her tone. *No. It's still September!*

She said, "I'm sorry. I've just been reading about manifestations—and conjuring."

"Your housewarming gift?"

"Aye. Yes. It came this morning. It's bonnie—beautiful, thank you."

"It is, but is it helpful?"

"I've worked out about conjuring, I think. Can you and Dellion do it?"

"Yes. Most fay can . . . or at least have the potential to. As you probably read, leprechauns almost never do, and galleonfee seldom, but that seems to be cultural rather than an innate lack of ability."

"Could I do it?"

"I'd say not. If you were able to, you probably would have by now."

"But I have a manifestation, and from what Branok said, that shouldn't be possible."

"He's right—but you see, it emerged on its own. You didn't expect it or court it or try to learn it."

"Mum and Dad don't even believe in it."

"That's the downside of being a trace fay," he said with seeming sympathy.

"Why doesn't the author, Piers le Fay, explain manifestations better?"

"Probably because none of us can."

"All he does is chunter on about *theories.* If he doesn't have an informed opinion—"

Andy laughed.

"What?"

"I daresay he has an informed opinion, but in proper scholarly fashion he chooses not to air it. He has a manifestation himself—quite a startling seasonal one."

"Like my curse? A Halloween occupation?"

"No, his is a Midsummer Knight mani—one of the few that's dangerous to the bearer. It afflicts courtfolk men almost exclusively, and only a few of them. Master le Fay is doubly unlucky in that his father is an elf man, but he threw hard to his mother's courtfolk blood."

That took the wind out of her sails.

She'd glanced at the book that explained the courtfolk, but she hadn't so far examined the one with elves.

"So the orders—is that the right term—they can—er—"

"Interbreed? Hybridise?"

She visualised Andy raising his fine brows, and then she flashed on Cousin Branok's annoyance when she'd mentioned green blood.

"I suppose so. Yes," she said.

"It would be odd if we couldn't," he said gently. "Considering you have a fay ancestor or so among the human majority, you must have realised it's possible, and indeed common for our people and yours, to make babies together."

"You and Dellion are of the same order."

"Yes, and so is Oliver."

Branok's partly human mother connected to Shane's side of the family. Yet Gillan was evidently pure—pisky, presumably.

Andy said, "Dellion and I have known one another since we were cradled. We always said if we didn't find anyone we liked better than one another by the time we were twenty, we'd marry. We didn't, so we did."

"Verra cosy, and a wee bit claustrophobic," Queenie muttered.

"It is and it isn't. But in any case, if one of us had found someone else, there's a good likelihood it would have been a pisky man or miss, even if we'd had to go hunting *over there.*"

"Why?"

"I believe volume four may explain that. But here's a clue—it's often said, of our order and even by us, that no one *but* a pisky man could ever survive living with a pisky miss. The only exception to that rule seems to be elves."

"What about you men?"

"Oh, we're reasonable, sweet, trusting—"

"—not to speak of abominably vain," Dellion's voice said.

"We have to be, to have the audacity to believe a pisky miss would have us and hold us and keep us without biting our head off," Andy continued. He went on, "I suggest you finish reading the books, Queenie. As I mentioned once already, you won't learn by osmosis."

Queenie managed to say a fairly civil goodbye before she hung up.

Usually, talking to Andy made her feel warmed and happy, but this time she just felt cross.

Dellion had suggested pisky men were vain, but Queenie considered *smug* was a better appellation. Andy Tredennick was a delightful young man . . . and smug.

She did as he suggested, though, and read some more of the books before turning to the back matter to read about the author and illustrator. It wasn't very informative, giving only a short paragraph on each.

Piers le Fay is a professor of history, originally from England. Some years ago, he moved to New South Wales, where he married his wife, Kendra.

The photograph showed a tall, rather beautiful fair-haired man, holding a delicately wrought helmet. He wore his hair a little longer than fashion dictated, and Queenie saw that his ears were slightly pointed. She assumed that denoted his elf heritage . . . she hadn't read much about the courtfolk, but she'd gathered the elves had pointed ears like the piskies.

She poured herself some coffee and made an online order of the supplies she needed for the festival.

It might be lucrative and was bound to be interesting, but she felt apprehensive about the affair. The Caledonian Curse was creeping in early.

Chapter Nineteen: Lassie Haggis

Queenie Hart. September, 2021

Queenie's latest order from Fiddle-de-Dee arrived promptly that afternoon.

As soon as she heard the motor turning into the circle, she took a deep breath and woke her mobile phone. She opened her gallery and looked earnestly at the photograph she'd taken of Mitch. True to form, she hadn't been able to bring his face to mind, but she found she recalled his presence quite well in other particulars. The features she'd described for him all came back to her.

Looking into his pictured face, she wondered again how she'd forgotten it. She'd caught him looking up enquiringly, with a half-smile.

His dark hair was a bit more than collar length, and his face had high cheekbones and an olive tone. His eyes were hazel, with long lashes and finely marked brows.

"Got you," she whispered. She kept her focus on the screen until the last possible moment when the knock came on the door. Then she opened the door with one hand and dropped her phone in her pocket with the other, lifting her gaze to look into the face she had forgotten already.

A young man's face looked back. He had brown hair and hazel eyes, and a fresh complexion. He smiled at her.

"Where's Mitch?" she asked, deflated and puzzled.

The lanky young man, probably no more than twenty-one, said, "Driving down to the station, I expect." He shifted his weight, and a strong waft of tomatoes came to her. He added, "I've brought your order, Mistress . . ." He paused, and then corrected himself. "Ms Hart."

"Thank you," she said listlessly. "Would you bring them in for me?"

"If you like." The young man carried a stack of boxes in through the arch.

Queenie indicated the kitchen, and he went on to arrange them on the bench.

He turned to her expectantly. "You're the Queen of Tarts."

"Aye—yes, so I am. Are you one of my customers?"

"Not yet. You'd sold out when I went to the market last week. My miss—my girlfriend—had a few things she needed me to do for her, and so I was late. Aunt Mim wasn't cross because she never is, but I think she'd be pleased if I could get some tarts today. Do you have any for sale?"

"I can let you have half a dozen," she said.

"Okay. Thanks." He felt in his pocket and took out a twenty. "Is this enough?"

"Plenty." She got him the tarts she'd intended to give to Mitch and handed over some change. "One of those is your free sample. If your aunt especially likes one kind, she can order more of that, or a mixture. I sell all sorts of combinations."

"Thank you," he said. He headed for the door and then turned to look back at her. "I'm Olivier, by the way."

She must have looked startled, because he made an enquiring face.

She replayed the name in her head. "Olivier," she said. "Not Oliver."

"I get that quite a lot," he said cheerfully. "Olivier Campania. I live at Fiddlers Rest—well, some of the time." He raised the hand that wasn't holding the box of tarts and took himself off.

Queenie went back to unpack her shopping. She still felt

oddly flat that Mitch hadn't come, but she tried to remember Olivier Campania's face, just to test herself.

It came easily to mind, pleasant and good-looking, and still touched with the mischief of the boy he'd been not very long ago.

She realised she'd seen him before. He was one half of the loved-up young couple she'd encountered down at the cove during her first visit to The Belfry. He'd had a second look at her then, and his girlfriend had objected.

Queenie sorted out her pantry and worked out probable orders for Oakengrove, as well as pre-orders from locals. And she mustn't forget Oliver Porthwellian's exacting expectations, either.

And Mitch. He was going to take her to the festival and bring her back. She'd pay him his going rate . . . whatever that was . . . but he was bound to want tarts. He always did.

She looked at his photo again.

How can I ever forget you? Why do I forget you? Auld Reekie, I even remember a delivery boy I've seen just once before! A delivery boy!

She chided herself, not only for the Caledonian slip, but also for her lack of respect.

So what if he's a delivery boy? He has a girlfriend and an aunt he clearly loves. Besides, Mitch is a delivery man, among other things, and I'm –

She sighed.

She was a lonely woman with a Scottish termagant waiting to take her over. She had three months of free rent—three months to make her reputation and to get solvent—and one of those months would be all but lost to her when she had to go into hibernation in a few days' time.

Then she lifted her chin.

I'm the Queen of Tarts. So I'd better get baking.

Queenie was up very early on the first morning of the

Oakengrove festival.

She had everything packed and waiting in the narthex well before six. Mitch had said he'd be busy driving all day, and she was determined not to take more of his time than necessary.

She'd used the tricycle successfully the week before, but there was no way it could manage the volume of stock she was taking to the festival.

When Mitch arrived, she put a box of tarts into his hands before either of them said a thing.

He popped the lid immediately and peeped inside.

His eyes rounded and he exhaled a gloating *ahhh.* He lifted out a tart with a crimped edge and a glowing red heart in its centre.

"That's the Queen of Hearts," she said.

He took a big bite and closed his eyes as he chewed. Then he looked at her directly, and said, "I thought that was *you.*"

"No, I'm just the Queen of Tarts."

"There's nothing *just* about you, Queenie Hart. You're magnificent, even if you do have flour on your chest. And so is this tart." He ate the rest of it while Queenie brushed at her shirt.

"Flour goes with the job," she said.

"I know. Are you ready?"

"Yes, all packed."

He picked up three of the boxes. "You hop in. I'll get these."

She went to the bus and got into her usual seat. He joined her seconds later.

"You didn't bring my groceries last time," she said, trying to sound neutral.

"I had another job on."

"Fixer or Driver?"

"Driver."

"You said you'd always come to me."

"If you want me, or need me, I will . . . but in this case you *needed* your flour and eggs and butter and vanilla . . . and it happened Olivier was the man of the hour because he was available, and I wasn't."

"You know him?"

"We both work casually for Fiddle-de-Dee. Nice lad."

"I gave him your tarts."

"Then what did I just eat?"

"That was a new batch. His aunt wanted some."

Mitch laughed. "Aunts should be given what they need."

"I wouldn't know. I've never had one."

"That's unfortunate."

She shrugged. "I have parents."

Mitch said, "So have I."

"Do they live locally?"

"Not really, although I see them a fair bit." He slowed the bus. "Here we are. Got your vendor's pass?"

"Yes."

"Know where you're setting up?"

"Nona sent me a schedule . . . she works here."

"So, where?" he prompted.

Queenie consulted the schedule and indicated the direction to take.

She showed her pass and was waved through.

Early as it was, some of the bands and vendors were already setting up. Queenie found her number on a small marquee which already bore a sign—*Queen of Tarts.*

"There's an ice chest where you can put your back-up trays for tomorrow," Mitch said.

Queenie nodded.

"Got plenty of those folding boxes?"

"Yes."

"Let's get you unloaded, then."

It took longer than usual, but eventually everything was ready. Mitch stood with his hands in his pockets looking about. "Good lineup of bands."

Queenie said, "I'm hoping to see the Dad Ballet."

"*Everyone* wants to see the Dads." He turned back to the bus. "I'll see you later, Queenie. What time do you want to be picked up?"

"What time suits you?"

"Nine."

She nodded. It was going to be a long day.

The first bands began playing at eight-thirty, half an hour after the festival opened to the public. As Oakengrove had large grounds, three or four acts could play at once, and the audience could move about as they pleased.

Business for Queenie was slow at first, but at around ten-thirty people started looking for morning tea, and quite a few chose the portable offerings over the sit-down cafes.

Queenie sold tarts to members of the audience and to some of the performers.

Most of them seemed to know one another. A tall young woman in tights and a jerkin, with a fiddle hitched to her back and a baby on her hip, stopped by, accompanied by an older woman in a steampunk costume. Incongruously, the second woman wore a baby sling in which reposed a small dog.

A handsome fair-haired man in troubadour's clothes hailed the pair. He was leading a horse on which a young woman sat side-saddle.

"Play with us, Elfie?" he called to the woman with the baby.

"Second set, then," called the violinist.

The girl on horseback raised a thumb in acknowledgement, and they went on.

A gaggle of men and women in military uniform streamed up and swarmed Queenie, pleading for tarts, *now,* because they had to be on in fifteen minutes and Isha was going to faint if she didn't get something sweet in her stomach.

Music from The Flying Fiddle heralded the beginning of the Dad Ballet setting up just opposite.

For a while, Queenie was able to enjoy the show in fits and starts as she served.

She'd known Bernie's troupe took their art seriously, but she was surprised at how accomplished they were.

The crowds thickened, blocking her view, and Queenie felt her good humour slipping a bit.

"Are these tarts dairy free?" a voice asked loudly.

It couldn't possibly be Angel Petty, but it sounded a lot like her.

"The ingredients of the different styles are on that chart," Queenie said. She pushed a leaflet towards the woman, whose nose was as sharp as her voice. "Here's a small version if you can't see over the crowd."

The woman ignored the leaflet.

"Never mind that, just tell me straight out. Are these ones dairy free?"

Queenie glanced at the tarts the woman was indicating. "No, that one has butter listed as one of the ingredients. The leaflet explains it."

"Yes, I know it has butter listed, but you can get dairy free butter."

"If I used margarine, I'd write margarine."

"Nut butter," said the woman.

"Butter is butter," Queenie said as patiently as she could.

"There are many different kinds of butters," the woman began to lecture.

"Aye, and I do use nut butters, in my chestnut and pecan tarts, and those are listed on the leaflets, but if it just says butter, it's just butter."

"You should specify that it's not dairy free instead of

expecting people to read your mind."

Queenie snapped. She put down the box she was packing for one of the Fusilier drummers and put her hands on her hips. "Wheest, ye auld besom, gie over, do!"

The contentious customer bristled. "What did you call me?"

"I'll call ye a wee cabbage-heided haggis if ye'll no' stop wi' the blether an' let me work!"

A small part of Queenie stood back, appalled at the invective coming from her mouth, but the larger part wished she had a tawse to lay on the auld besom's arse to teach her some manners.

For a few seconds things hung in the balance, and then the young woman on the horse, who had completed her circuit of the grounds and who had been watching with a grin, slid down from her mount and advanced on Queenie.

She was small, with a lot of long brown hair and a bewilderingly frilled and tucked smock that swung around her neat calves.

She gave the angry woman a smart pat on the shoulder. "I think you ought to listen to t' baker. She knows her business, and you're disrupting it." She had an odd accent that Queenie thought was northern English . . . possibly from Yorkshire or Lancashire.

It might have been her words and tone, but it was more likely the horse capering behind her that dispersed the crowd out to the sides.

The young woman turned and swatted the horse on the nose. "Give over, Art! Court, thou great gaby, get—"

The fair man, grinning, took charge of the horse. Then he retreated, backwards.

The woman turned back to the complainer. "If thou't knows what good for thee, shut thy gob and git!"

She turned and came to put a comforting arm around

Queenie's shoulders, having to reach up to do it. "Art all reet, lass?"

Queenie hauled her vocabulary back to its normal range. "Yes, thanks," she muttered. She was very much ashamed.

"Best sit down." The young woman pressed her into a chair. "Daft old gooby," she added, though she didn't seem to mean Queenie.

The fiddler with the baby had returned. She fixed her gaze on the man with the horse. "Court?"

He shrugged, still grinning. "I think my wife's got it in hand, Elfie."

"Probably." Elfie stepped forward into the now clear marquee and asked, politely, "Is there any chance of buying some tarts, or would you rather we all went away while you recover from—er—"

"She's got a radged braewoman in her," the younger girl said.

"Oh?" The fiddler looked interested.

"Takes one to know one . . . only Tansy's got a doughty wench, haven't you, my lovely?" the horse man said.

"Say that more and I'll let her loose to pink thy arse," Tansy said cheerfully. She turned back to Queenie. "All right now, lovie? We can stay if you like and keep the scratchy old cats away."

Queenie was glad of her support, but she knew it was up to her to get out of the mess.

"Thanks . . . um—"

"Tansy Leopold," the woman said.

"Thanks, Tansy. I'm sorry for making a scene."

"Tansy loves a good scene," her husband said. He cocked his head. "But if you're okay, we'd probably better get back to Cathie before we do our second set. She's our daughter, and she's probably doing something terrible to Joss."

"I'll be fine," Queenie said.

Who the hell is Joss?

The girl gave her a pat. "Nowt to worry."

The fiddler said, hopefully, "Tarts?"

Queenie pulled herself together. "Yes. Sorry. Better get some before someone comes to throw me out for raising a riot."

The steampunk woman said, "I think you'll be okay, love. You didn't throw things, and I doubt Missus Buttercup had a clue what you were saying. What *were* you saying?"

"Scotch," one of the military singers said, returning to the marquee.

"Scotch burble," another of them continued, enlarging on the joke.

"It's a dialect known as *lassie haggis,*" the tallest of them said, grinning.

Queenie offered them each a promotional tart, but inside she felt cold.

The dairy-free woman might complain about her to the Oakengrove committee, and if she did, it would be goodbye to coming back tomorrow, let alone next year, and goodbye to her hope of selling her wares directly to the estate to serve in their in-house café.

I shouldnae ha' come.

"No, you *really* should not," Queenie murmured, as she continued packing tarts for the drummer.

The steampunk woman asked if she ever made cheese tarts. "Pepe is partial to a bit of cheese."

"Pepe's Nell's chihuahua," the military bandsman said helpfully.

Queenie said, "I have some I call Cheesy Grins. They're cream cheese. He might like those, but I'm not sure if pastry is good for wee dogs."

"Bless you, Pepe's as old as the hills. A little of what he fancies keeps him interested in life."

Queenie handed over the box and then she found a slightly battered Cheesy Grin. "If you'll be here tomorrow, I can bring some savoury tarts."

"We'll be here," the steampunk woman said.

Queenie just hoped she would be, too.

Chapter Twenty: Supper with the Fixer

Queenie Hart. September, 2021

By the time Mitch arrived to take her home, Queenie was weary beyond belief. It was the longest market day she'd ever put in, and the strain of keeping the Caledonian Curse suppressed exhausted her. Despite the support she'd had from the eccentric onlookers, she feared her outburst of *lassie haggis* would have severe repercussions.

The customer is always right.

Even when one is being obnoxious?

Even then.

Mitch seemed tired, too.

When Queenie, not recognising him because she wasn't really expecting him, handed him a leaflet, telling him she had no gluten free or dairy free left, he said quietly, "It's me, Queenie."

He pulled a Fixer cap from somewhere and crammed it onto his head.

"Oh!" Queenie was almost ready to sob with mortification.

"Are you ready?" he asked.

She nodded.

"The bus is just over there. Hop in."

"I have to pack up."

"It can be left safely. The tarts for tomorrow will be better off if you leave them in the cool chest rather than carry them about. Bring just what you need tonight and for the morning.

I'll ward up the marquee."

Queenie picked up a few items and went obediently to the bus.

They drove the short distance to The Belfry in silence.

"You're quiet," Mitch said. "Did it go well, today?"

"I insulted a customer."

He said, "I expect he deserved it."

"She. It was an auld besom havering on about dairy free."

"Whatever for? Tarts are commonly made with butter."

"Mm." She felt Caledonia calling, and hardly dared to say more.

Mitch pulled into Kirk Circle and stopped near the curve of the wall. "Are you going straight to bed?" he asked.

Queenie shook her head.

"You should. You look tired."

"So do you."

"I'll manage. What do you need to do?"

What *did* she need to do? She knew there was something.

And then she remembered.

"I promised a customer I'd have savoury tarts tomorrow for her wee dog."

"You can't make those tonight. You'd fall asleep in the pastry, and they'd burn."

Queenie felt tears prickling.

I shouldnae promise what I cannae deliver.

"I have an idea. Why not make the pastry tonight and let it rest while you get some sleep? In the morning, you can fill and bake. Do you have the ingredients to hand? If not, I can fix that."

"Aye, but—" She broke off. "I *could* do that. I'd be late at the festival, but business was no so brisk until mid-morning . . ."

"Then that's what we'll do." Mitch sprang out of the bus and came around to help Queenie down. He kept hold of her hand as they entered The Belfry, and she hadn't the energy or the will to reject him.

"You start the pastry, and I'll get supper," he said.

Obediently, Queenie set to with flour and butter. She heard Mitch switch on the jug, and then he rattled about with mugs and spoons.

When she turned to refresh her memory of his face, he was stirring something in a shallow pan over the stove.

"What are you doing?"

He glanced sideways at her. "Heating soup."

"Where—"

"It's some I made last night. Mum's recipe. There are some sourdough rolls from Daily Bread in my bag."

Queenie finished the pastry and set it to rest.

She discovered Mitch had commandeered two of the black-patterned bowls and some spoons.

"Eat this, and then we'd better get some sleep," he said. He moved to sit opposite her at the tiny kitchen table. "If I sit here, you won't get a crick in your neck glancing at me every time you forget what the strange man in your kitchen looks like."

Queenie felt her cheeks heating in a miserable blush. Unwilling to look at him after that, she kept her focus on the soup. It was good, and so were the bread rolls.

She finished up and then risked a look.

He was chewing the last piece of bread. He reached across for her bowl, stacked it in his, and took them across to the sink.

"Just a rinse, then it's bedtime."

She got to her feet, swaying, ready to see him to the door.

Instead, she heard herself say, "Laddie, I'd like it fine if ye'd stay the nicht."

He froze for a second and then he said, "That seems practical. I can be cook's assistant in the morning. Do you want me to sleep in the chair?"

"It's a gey big bed," she said with a shrug.

"You turn in, then. I'll rinse these bowls."

Queenie disbelieved the whole scene, but she was too tired to explain herself, and she thought it would be impossible anyway. She had a wash and cleaned her teeth, untied her hair, undressed, and pulled on the old t-shirt she wore as a nightie.

She climbed the shallow steps to the mezzanine bedroom and tumbled into bed.

The springy, hay-scented mattress welcomed her, and her bamboo pillow cradled her aching head.

She was almost asleep when she felt the mattress dip as Mitch got in beside her. He smelled of soap and toothpaste, and she wondered if he'd borrowed her toothbrush. She tried to feel indignant, but it didn't seem worth the effort.

She felt the bed rock as he leaned over her. He kissed her cheek gently. "Goodnight, queen of my heart."

There's a terrible line . . .

She was asleep.

In the morning, she woke with a feeling of urgency.

Something had to be dealt with, quickly, before—

The sound of the jug bubbling came to her, and she smelled toast and strawberries.

Careful footsteps on the stair made her sit up in a hurry as a strange man appeared, face-first, and then shoulders and—a breakfast tray.

Queenie stared uncomprehendingly for a second before it fell into place.

This was Mitch Kingsolver, the Fixer, who had driven her home and spent the night.

"Good morning, Queenie," he said, sliding the tray onto the bedside table. "Tea and cheese on toast and a bit of fruit. Don't worry, it's not *your* cheese. It's a nice goat cheese my mother makes. She keeps goats, you see."

She blinked. "Thank you."

"I could have been corny and stuck a rose on the tray. But it's a bit too early in the season, so you'll have to make do with a daffodil."

Queenie pushed back her hair, looking anywhere but at him.

"I have someone to get from Borrow, but I'll be back to be cook's helper by the time you've had a shower."

He turned without waiting for an answer and started down the steps.

Queenie wanted to yell after him to ask if he'd borrowed her toothbrush again this morning, but as she couldn't recall his face, it didn't seem right.

She knew she should feel horribly startled and uneasy about sharing a bed with a man whose face she seemed unable to learn, but she couldn't manage it.

They'd both been far too tired to share anything *but* the bed. It had been a practical solution.

She started eating breakfast, but she had to pause halfway through to dig out her phone and open the photograph that was fast becoming her lifeline.

Fifteen minutes later, she was showered and down in the kitchen prepping her tarts. There wasn't enough time to do anything fancy, so she decided on Cheese Bubbles, Moon Tarts and Tomato Fans. Surely one of these would please an elderly wee dog who deserved indulgences.

Mitch came back in time to slice tomatoes with a sharp paring knife and to beat up eggs and black pepper while she diced and melted cheese.

"Green cheese?" he asked as she mixed minced parsley in with one batch.

"Close. Moon Tarts. Och—Guid Laird!"

"What's the matter?"

"I've forgotten Oliver's wee order! He'll be fashed."

"Who's Oliver?"

Queenie explained her special customer as well as the encroaching Caledonian Curse would allow.

"You'd better send him six of these and put a note in to say the balance will be with him tomorrow. He can't want to eat the whole dozen in one day."

You would, she thought but she said, "He's no' had cheese tarts before."

"He'll love them. There's not a man alive who could resist your tarts. Have you thought of ranging the sizes? Wee tarts for wee appetites through to muckle tarts for hungry ladies?"

"Is that a wee bitty hint?"

He laughed. "Rumbled. But I can wait for what I want, as long as I have what I need."

The first batch was in the oven faster than Queenie anticipated. It helped a lot to have someone else doing part of the preparation, and she even had time to make up a hurried list of ingredients for her leaflets. No time to update the big wall chart, but the leaflets would do for today.

The bus pulled up at the Oakengrove gates at nine-thirty. Queenie half-expected to be turned away after the dairy-free incident, but Nona, who was checking passes, waved her through with a cheerful *good morning, love.*

It seemed to be a *thing* in Fiddle Bay, to call folk *love.* Duncan Dee from the supermarket did it. Maureen did it. Even Mitch did it sometimes.

Mitch got her set up in his usual lightning fashion, turned, and jumped back into the bus.

Queenie dropped the leaflets she was setting out and ran to intercept him, banging on the driver's window with her fist as he started the engine.

He looked down at her. "Did I forget something?"

"Aye!" She breathed out hard, crushing Caledonia as hard as she could. "No," she said quietly. "I wanted to say thank you before you got away."

He smiled. "It's not—"

"Altruism. I know. It's what you do. But a few tarts isn't much in exchange for all you do . . . considering you haven't even got them yet."

The sudden wicked glint in his hazel eyes gave her just a half-second warning before he leaned out and murmured, "Aye, love, but I got to spend the night in bed with the Queen of Tarts. That's got to be an expensive luxury—"

"Wha' a dreadfu' thing tae say! Ye horrid wee haggis! Wheesht! Where's a besom when I need it—" She slapped both hands over her mouth.

The Fixer stared down at her with lively delight.

Then he put the bus into gear. "I'll pick you up at ten, love. If you want me earlier, call me and I'll come." He drove away.

Queenie heard a gasp behind her. She turned quickly to face the delivery lad from Fiddle de Dee. He had one arm around his dark-haired silver-hung girl, and one hand over her mouth.

The girl pried his hand away, turned it and kissed the wrist. Then she said to Queenie, "He wouldn't let me applaud you, the brute. What *did* your man say to you to bring that on?"

Queenie didn't feel like repeating it, so she said, randomly, "Like a tart?"

The girl laughed. "*Bleddy hell!* That'd do it."

"We would," the boy said. He scented the air like a hungry hound. "Do I smell cheese and parsley?"

Queenie sold out by the end of the afternoon, but she didn't call Mitch the Fixer. She wasn't sure she'd ever want to face him again.

She watched the Dad Ballet and some of the other acts and familiarised herself with the grounds of Oakengrove.

The man with the horse and the small outspoken wife

turned out to be one half of the act called *Courtesan*, which she recalled Mitch mentioning as one of the better-known bands remaining faithful to Oakengrove.

The other half of the act was a serene-faced alto named Jordana. Their chemistry onstage was electric, but it was clearly stage-only, because they were both married to other people.

The fiddle player with the baby girl was there, and her steampunk friend, who had already bought some of the savoury tarts, came over and asked for an order form.

"I'd like a couple of orders a month . . . no, three," she said.

"For your wee dog?"

The woman slid a hand into the sling to caress the snoozing chihuahua. "A piece of cheese tart will be coming his way for his suppers, but I want some for my man . . . and my grandkids. Petra, my daughter, doesn't hold with sweets for the kids, but *I* tell her they *will* eat something more than fruit and veggies so better train them with good wholesome things rather than packaged muck. Pardon my French. Have you ever thought of doing a vegetable tart option? I've heard you can make a kind of tart base with cauliflower rice, though you'd have to eat it with a fork—"

Queenie handed over a form. She wasn't sure about cauliflower rice, but flower tarts . . . candied rose petals for Valentine's Day would be fun.

The woman said, "No flak from the Missus Buttercup incident I hope?"

"Not so far."

"She's probably simmered down. If she's got any sense, she'll have noticed public opinion was against her."

"I shouldna' hae—I shouldn't have said it, though."

"You shouldn't, for your sake rather than hers. But you know the adage—sticks and stones."

Queenie sighed, hardly daring to speak. The adage cut both ways.

The woman filled out the form and lettered in her name. *Nell Andover.*

As Mitch said, there were a few ways to learn someone's identity without asking for it . . .

Chapter Twenty-one: Caledonia on My Mind

Queenie Hart. September, 2021

It was dark.

Queenie *struck camp,* as she thought of it, carefully collating order forms for the month ahead in order of delivery.

Folk will have to collect them from outside The Belfry.

She'd ordered a kind of delivery hatch from a local woodturner. She hoped it would be ready in time.

Maureen and Nona came by, and Maureen's friendly seagull gaze zeroed in on the empty trays and boxes. She handed Queenie a sheet of paper with the *Stradevarious* letterhead.

"What's this for?" Queenie asked, tired and a bit confused.

"This is me wearing my editor hat, love," Maureen said.

"Mum, can't it wait?" Nona had a paper of her own. "This is a questionnaire, Queenie. Not my doing—the Oakengrove management like to get feedback from new vendors and acts. No hurry, but it would be useful if you could fill it in sometime. Just your impressions and suggestions."

Maureen said, "Cheeky. I was first. Queenie, we're putting a special *Strad* out to showcase the Experience. We don't want essays or blatant puff pieces, but any funny story that can naturally mention your stall is welcome."

Queenie folded the questionnaire and the *Strad* address together and slid them into her apron pocket. "I will . . . and thank you."

"What for?" Nona asked.

"Everything. Helping me to get this stall. Advertising that I won't be at the market next month."

Maureen said, "The bay is a friendly place, but it operates on a reciprocal system. Bernie reckons if we go that extra mile, or let that tiny slight pass by without reacting—"

"That doesn't mean you should put up with deliberate obstruction," Nona said.

"You heard about Ms Dairy-free, then," Queenie said.

"Who hasn't?"

"Did she complain about me?"

Nona said, slowly, "She tried it on, but a few folk who witnessed the incident went in to bat for you, and since their goodwill is of more lasting value to the Experience than one disgruntled visitor's . . . that's not to say you get out of gaol free. Management suggested you might need to bring an assistant next year to avoid sensory overload stress."

"Lot of modern nonsense," Maureen said.

Nona shrugged.

"I will be allowed to come next year then?" Queenie asked.

"Oh, yes. Queen of Tarts features high in the Vox Pol Box from yesterday. *Nice alternative to ultra-healthy and junk* is the consensus."

Maureen asked, "Are you right for getting home?"

"Yes—Mitch is coming for me."

Nona grinned at her. "Nice one. You know what they say about men's hearts and stomachs . . ."

"It doesn't hurt when you're also easy on the eye," Maureen said.

"Mum!" Nona towed her mother away.

Queenie folded up the small table that belonged with the marquee. Then she opened her phone.

"Remember me?"

She looked up sharply into Mitch's friendly gaze. He was

standing a couple of metres away, holding one of his caps, and he slowly tossed it to land at her feet.

"What's that for?" Queenie asked.

"Tossing my hat into the ring to see if you'd swat it. You didn't, so I hope I'm forgiven?"

"I hope *I* am," she muttered.

"Nothing to forgive, love. I pushed your buttons and got the serve that was coming to me. Into the bus and I'll get your stuff packed."

When he slid in beside her a minute later, she said, "How do you *do* that? And don't say *what*."

"It's what I do."

"I know, but *how*?"

He turned the bus carefully and joined the slow exodus from the grounds of Oakengrove.

"Part of being a Fixer?" Queenie asked.

"If you like." He added, "If you want to remember my face, you might print your photo on a t-shirt or something. Then you'd just have to look down at yourself."

"I wear my Queen of Tarts t-shirt when I'm working."

"I've noticed. It seems to attract flour."

She brushed at herself.

The Belfry was in sight within minutes, and Queenie gathered herself to alight.

Mitch stopped the bus in the usual place. "You go on ahead, and I'll fetch your things in."

She nodded. He wasn't going to help her out of the bus tonight.

By the time she had the jug on, everything was neatly stacked in the kitchen.

She turned to face him. He glanced away towards the foyer—no, the narthex—and shifted his cap in his fingers.

"Mitch."

He looked back at her. "Forgotten my face again?"

"Not now I'm looking at you. I'm in a fix."

He nodded. "I can see that."

"Well—get me out of it. That's what you do."

"It is, but in this case, you have to take the first step. Ask, I mean."

"I just did."

"Specifically."

Queenie squirmed. She felt a surge of lassie haggis invective rising, but she caught it in time. "You stayed with me last night. We were both tired, and I didn't like to think of you driving home to wherever you live. Where *do* you live?"

"I have two places. One's the place where I go when I have time on my hands, which isn't often. The other is a *pied-à-terre* in Borrow—though it's my main place at present."

"Oh."

He raised his brows. "Why? Did you think I camped out in Ethel?"

"No—" Though she had wondered. If he could afford *two* places, driving and fixing and delivering must pay better than she'd have expected.

"I have a housemate," he added.

"Oh."

"Her name's Ayesha, and she likes to wake me by patting my cheek."

"Oh."

"With her paw," he added, deadpan.

"She's a cat."

"Yes, a silver tabby . . . an ice queen. She's the original cat-who-walks, which is handy, because she doesn't always insist on my constant presence. In fact, I sometimes get the idea I'm a great inconvenience to her because I disrupt her routine."

"I'd have taken you for a dog person."

"I'm between dogs at present. Ayesha has made her stipulations plain."

"Would Ayesha allow you to spend another night with me?"

"Will you threaten me with a besom if I tell you I've been home to feed her and to set up her favourite music earlier this evening on the off-chance you might invite me?"

"About the besom—"

"I can go home if you prefer."

Queenie said, "I'd like some company tonight. There are some things I want to explain to you, before—"

"Before October comes," he put in.

"Yes. How did you know?"

"Takes one to know one. That's a cliché, but it's true. I have things to tell you about October. I should have done it before."

She puffed out her cheeks. "I have some salad things in the fridge, and you can get a towel out of the cupboard in the bathroom. I'll get supper ready. You get first shower."

"So—you'll share a bed with me, but you're not ready to share a shower."

"That's it."

"Make sure you open that picture when you hear the water turn off. You don't want to meet a naked stranger on the stairs." He turned and headed for the bathroom.

Queenie put supper together. She did as Mitch suggested, and had the photo up when he returned, not naked as threatened, but a wee bit damp around the edges and wearing an obviously clean shirt. It was rather an odd one, dull green with leather lacing up the front. The lacing was loose, showing a handspan of broad chest.

"Your turn," he said.

Queenie looked back into his face, experiencing the usual jolt of belated recognition.

Then she ducked off to the bathroom and cleaned up.

By the time she returned, Mitch had added more soup to the supper things. They ate in companionable silence, and then he rinsed off the plates and turned to take her hand. "Ready for bed?"

She kept her gaze on his face. "Yes, but don't think—"

"I don't *think* anything, love. You wanted some company, and I'm it. Do you want to have our wee talk tonight in bed, or should we wait until morning?"

"That depends. Do you have to be up at crack of dawn to drive someone somewhere?"

"Not until ten. The festival people usually spend that long getting debriefed."

"Good." She went with him up the shallow steps, pleased the flight was broad enough for them to walk side-by-side.

Queenie took off her gown and tossed it over a chair before hesitating.

T-shirt on or off?

She glanced back at Mitch, zeroing in on his face as usual. It was as well she did, because he had his clothes off . . . every stitch.

"Losh!" She looked away in a hurry.

"Not cool?" he asked.

"Crivvens!"

"That's hardly fitting for a church, queen of my heart."

"What—"

"It's derived from *Christ help me,* I think. I can put something back on if you want, although I usually don't wear clothes to bed. Your bed. Your rules. I shouldn't have assumed."

Caledonia simmered, but Queenie made an effort. "Just get in, please."

He got in.

She got in, and they lay side by side.

Mitch put his hands behind his head, apparently happy and relaxed. "Are you going to put the light out?"

"I was wondering whether to risk it."

"You don't want to find yourself in the arms of a man

whose face you can't remember."

"No."

"It wasn't a problem last night."

"Last night I was too tired to think. And there was no question of *arms*."

"Is there tonight?"

"I'm thinking."

"About my ill-timed quip about spending the night with the Queen of Tarts, I expect. Will a heartfelt apology cut it?"

"No, because you wouldn't mean it. You knew exactly what you were saying."

"And you were into the *thanking* again."

"Don't you like to be thanked?"

"I don't need thanking. It's what I do."

"Is *this* what you do?"

"Not usually."

"Explain that."

"A couple of years back . . . someone was in a fix, and I helped her out. Her husband had died after a long bout with some disease or other, and she was hurting. She was mourning him sincerely, but the family—his family—expected her to—"

"Go full-on Queen-Victoria-Widow-of-Windsor."

"Yes. So I spent some nights with her—when the loneliness was too crushing."

"And?"

"And, after a while, she explained very nicely to her in-laws that she was still above ground, and although she had a forever diamond on her finger, she wanted children before she was too old. And before you jump to conclusions, she didn't want them with me. I look a bit like her husband, you see, sometimes, and she wanted her children to look decidedly unlike him, so she wouldn't be reminded of what might have been. I introduced her to a lovely guy from the islands.

He's dark-skinned with blue eyes. He was happy to provide what she termed a *baby-starter,* but he said she had to have him around as part of the package to finish what he'd started. He was willing to plant a baby, but he was going to be around to rear the child, even if its mother didn't want him as her husband. Cue fireworks." He chuckled. "I had them both bending my ears there for a while about how unreasonable the other was being."

"What happened?"

"I don't know, love. I told them they had to fix *that* one themselves. They both got the hump with me, and I haven't heard from them since. But, since I seldom think of them, I assume they're fixed. If they weren't, they'd be bothering at the back of my mind."

"I see."

"That's the only time I've done that style of fixing."

"Except for now."

"This isn't that. Not fixing. You were in a fix, but you don't need *fixing.* I'm here because you asked, and because I want to be."

Queenie digested this. She rolled on her side and considered his profile. "Maybe we could leave the light on *dim,* so I don't wake up and have a conniption."

"Strange naked man in bed."

"Yes." She stretched out one foot and poked his leg. "If we get as far as the arms bit, I want to go on top. That way I can see your face, but you won't be looming at me."

"You'll loom at me instead."

"You're welcome to close your eyes."

"And miss the expression on your face when you go wide-mouthed with ecstasy?"

"You have a grand opinion of your prowess, laddie."

"I do, that. I suppose kissing is out?"

"I don't know. I wouldn't be able to see you."

"You can put your fingers on my face to remind you. Braille me."

She reached out and traced his features. "It might work. If it doesn't, and if I scream and go lassie haggis on you, then I beg forgiveness in advance."

"I hope you will scream . . . or at least give a little satisfied murmur."

She moved closer and kissed his cheek.

He put his arms loosely around her. "I li—"

Queenie cut him off as her body suddenly took over and she pressed urgently against him, closing her mouth over his.

What about—

Och, it's all right. He's no' putting it about.

She kept her hands on his face as he helped her to roll on top of him.

His arms firmed around her, and he got his hands under the shirt and stroked her back.

"When you're ready," he murmured, muffled against her lips.

Queenie quivered. She should raise her head to check on his face, but instead, she tucked her face into his shoulder, kissing the warm skin. He smelled gently of eucalyptus.

I could make eucalyptus tarts . . . with honey . . .

Losh!

An electric pulse seemed to run through her as her thoughts fled south.

She squirmed against him, mouth open, back arching as pleasure pulsed through her.

She gasped again and went limp.

He said, breathlessly, "Could you please—"

"Och! No' finished yet laddie?" She brought her attention back where it ought to be, then sat up so she could see his face.

He had his eyes closed in concentration, and she admired his long eyelashes until they lifted as his eyes opened wide, and she saw his pupils had all but swallowed the hazel colour.

She tightened her thighs and bore down, feeling him tense and then relax beneath her.

They stared at one another and then Queenie said, "Oops. You're not wearing—"

"No need. You're safe from consequences. Physical ones."

"Are you sure?"

"Would I have let you have me if I wasn't?"

"Let, is it?" She pouted at him. "Besides, there's a physical consequence, and it's going to be all over my sheets."

He extracted one hand from under the sheet and held out a handkerchief. "Best I can do. It's clean."

"What about you?"

"I have another one."

"Right. Yes. On the count of three, then."

They counted down and uncoupled. Queenie flopped down beside him, still watching his face.

Now we'll have that talk about October.

However, they didn't. He finished mopping up, rolled to face her and offered his arms.

"What if I wake up and—"

"Then I'll remind you. Are you a morning glory person?"

She chuckled. "That's for me to know and you to find out."

She snuggled against him. A voice at the back of her mind said this was a bad idea. In just a few days' time she'd have to isolate herself, so starting something with Mitchell Kingsolver right now was irresponsible.

Och, I can tell him in the morning. Maybe he'll understand . . .

On the edge of sleep, she heard a strange fluttering sound. It seemed to come from the belltower.

About the Author

Lark Westerly lives in the island state of Tasmania.

Like Queenie Hart, she often thinks Obsession might be her extra middle name. Some of her obsessions include creating worlds, lists of interesting names, walking the dogs, reading, and pursuing whatever research might support her current project. For Queen of Tarts, she read up on Scottish dogs, the expenses involved in hiring a piper, Cornish names, Picts, brocade, Scottish slang, English names, name frequency tables, church terminology and Scotch Broth. She had a great deal of fun meeting old friends, and being quite startled to realise that telephoning Dellion Tredennick, eating tarts with Queenie, and buying a costume from Fairings after a visit to the O-Quay Café really wasn't on the cards tomorrow.

She *has* been to Circular Quay, but there wasn't a living statue, and he didn't give her a wish.

www.ingramcontent.com/pod-product-compliance
Lightning Source LLC
Chambersburg PA
CBHW060822120626
46557CB00001B/330

* 9 7 8 1 4 8 7 4 3 4 5 0 2 *